PAY FOR YOU

This book is a work of fiction.

Names, characters, organisations, places, events and incidents are either products of the author's imagination or are used fictitiously.

Colin J Galtrey books available on Amazon worldwide in Kindle and Paperback formats

John Gammon Series One
Book One: Things Will Never Be the Same Again
Book Two: Sad Man
Book Three: Joy Follows Sorrow
Book Four: Never Cry On A Bluebell
Book Five: Annie Tanney

John Gammon Series Two
Book One: The Poet and the Calling Card
Book Two: Why
Book Three: Your Past Is your Future
Book Four: Intravenous
Book Five: The Sorrow Begins

PAY FOR YOUR SIN

John Gammon Series Three ✹ ✹ ✹

Book One: The Magpie
Book Two: The Cure
Book Three: Body Parts
Book Four: Pay For Your Sin

Alternative Genres from Colin J Galtrey

The Shona Trilogy

Book One: Looking For Shona
Book Two: The Hurt of Yochana
Book Three: Grove

Stand Alone Books

Got To Keep Running: Saskia Wagers is on the run her life is in terrible danger. Will she survive?

I Am Fawn Jones: A crime involving an eccentric man whose fascination with the after-life may help solve a case. Do you believe in the after-life? You may well do after reading this book!

Scarab Falls: Set in 1970s Ireland during the troubles. Two young men who think they are invincible until they cross the IRA. The story takes one of the young men to London, Staffordshire, Channel Islands and a Scottish Island.

PAY FOR YOUR SIN

Contents

With John Gammon's friend and lover murdered, revenge was on his mind constantly with the two murders still not solved, Helen Spirios and DI Sandra Scooper were starting to haunt him.

John knew all the accolades he received as DCI Gammon would be short-lived if he didn't at least find Sandra's murderer.

In this third series the newly promoted Detective Chief Inspector John Gammon is desperate to do well now that he has achieved the rank he wanted. Now he had to prove to his peers and himself that he had the ability to do the job.

PAY FOR YOUR SIN

CHAPTER ONE

At times John wondered if this was the life he wanted. He stood in his office looking toward Losehill. The spectacular view always seemed to inspire him, but it wasn't having that effect today. He had Sandra's and Helen Spiros's murders to solve and the trail was totally cold. John Glew had taken his own life and was the actual perpetrator of the whole carnage that Ugis Bravas carried out. And now he had just been told Bravas was to be taken back to Bulgaria. It left a bitterness he knew he had to overcome.

Lady Hasford had sold up and moved to Cornwall with Rosie. A friend of Cheryl's had bought Sandra's place which Saron was a bit miffed about. Not that she had told John, she was still very cold towards him. He had heard no more from Anouska and baby Anka, but he sent money every month to support her.

Then there was Fleur Dubois his sister, he had heard nothing for four months now. John was finding the DCI job came with a lot of politics and paperwork, luckily he had a good team round him. DI Lee and DI Smarty were both working on a case which he had yet to get too involved in.

Chief Inspector Sim was turning out to be a good ally for Gammon, but Gammon did think that Andrew Sim was pleased that Ugis Bravas was being deported back to Bulgaria. There was something fishy about DCI Dirk and why he was murdered. It suited the force for the case to be taken out of the limelight so to speak.

Gammon's phone rang and in his current state of mind he was pleased to see it was his mate Steve Lineman.

"Morning mate, how are you?"

PAY FOR YOUR SIN

"Good Steve, what's up?"

"Nothing mate, just wondered if you fancied popping down for a pint to the Star tonight?"

"Can do mate, should be in about 6.00pm, it's quiet at the moment."

Gammon had no sooner got the words out of his mouth when Milton popped his head round the door.

"Steve, I will see you about 6.00pm, somethings just come up."

"Yes Carl, can I help?"

"Sorry Sir, but we have a man downstairs that says he came home and his wife was dead in the living room. I have sent forensics and DS Bass and DI Kiernan have gone to the house also."

"Ok Carl, is the man in the incident room?"

"Yes Sir."

"Ok, let's go and have a chat."

Gammon entered the room with Milton. The man was in his mid-forties slightly balding with glasses that reminded Gammon of the Joe 90 character. He had a cream coloured mac so Gammon thought he was maybe an office worker?

"Ok, Mr?"

"Lord, Cuthbert Lord."

"May I call you Cuthbert?"

"Yes, not a problem."

"Would you like to tell me what happened?"

"I had left for the office this morning."

"Where do you work?"

"Stacey and Lord Solicitors."

"Are you a partner?"

"Yes, I am."

"Anyway, I always make a mixed fruit drink and take it to work, but I forgot to pick it up off the side this morning. We are quiet at work and it's only about thirty minutes from Cramford to Pritwich, so I drove back to get it. That's when I found my wife. The back door had been forced but Amy was still in bed. I tried to wake her and rolled her over, and she had got one of our kitchen knives in her chest. I think it was into her heart, that's when I saw all the blood. I felt her pulse but couldn't feel one, so I called an ambulance and came here to report it."

"Mr Lord, this is said with the greatest respect, but you appear very matter of fact about the death of your wife."

"She always said I didn't show my feelings, Mr Gammon."

"Did your wife have any enemies that you know of?"

"Amy, enemies? No everybody loved Amy. She was a nursery nurse at Ackbourne Flip Flops as it's called."

"Ok Mr Lord, DI Milton will take details and arrange for any counselling or help you may need. I will be in touch. Sorry for your loss."

Gammon had seen some characters in his time, but this guy was coolness personified. He had just lost his wife and it was like he had dropped fifty pence down a drain.

"DI Lee, come with me. Let's go and see where Amy Lord worked. I will explain on the way."

Gammon and Lee arrived at Flip Flops Nursery.

"Good morning, DCI Gammon and DI Lee."

They flashed their warrant cards.

"I believe Amy Lord worked here as a Nursery Nurse, is that correct?"

"Yes, she still does."

PAY FOR YOUR SIN

"I'm afraid she was found murdered today."

"Oh, no."

The stout lady sat down quite shocked.

"Are you the owner?"

"Yes, Ann Springlow. What happened?" It was Amy's day off today."

"Was Amy well liked?"

"Kind of, Mr Gammon."

"That sounds to me like not by everyone."

"Well she could be flirty, and some of the girls didn't like that. I shouldn't speak ill of the dead, but rumour was she was having an affair."

"Do you have a name for us?"

"Well I don't want to get anybody into trouble."

"It may be very important."

"A guy called Tommy Spire from Pritwich."

"Do you know anything else about Mr Spire?"

"All I heard was he is on the board at Pippa's Frozen Foods at Lingcliffe, but that's all I know."

"Did Mr Lord know?"

"I'm not sure."

"Ok, here is my card Ann, if you can think of anything give me a call."

Gammon and Lee left for Bixton.

"We will go up to see Mr Spire in the morning, after we have some information from Wally from the meeting tomorrow."

Gammon called it a night mindful Steve had asked him for a drink at the Star in Puddle Dale. John drove down through the quaint village of Puddle Dale with its old stocks still intact on the village green, and its walled sheep dip. Although no longer used, the villagers kept it clean. John

PAY FOR YOUR SIN

pulled into the Star Inn car park and at the back of the car park John could see work had begun on the outbuildings.

As he entered the bar Steve was sitting at the bar talking to Imogen, with just one old lad and a dog sat by the fire.

"Evening."

"Hey mate good to see you."

"He didn't get the same vibe from Imogen, but he could have been imagining it.

"Get John a pint of Star Ale, please sweetheart."

"So mate, going to cut straight to the chase, will you be my best man?"

"What? That's a bit sudden, Steve."

"After losing Jo and our little girl I never thought I would be happy again, and Imogen lights up my life, John."

"Well if you are sure, you know I am happy for you mate. And of course I will be your best man. When is the wedding?"

"Near Christmas we think, so about four months away, John."

"Best get a new suit then mate."

"No, it's top hat and tails mate. Marrying at St James Church in Puddle Dale. We are having the wedding party here at the Star."

"Ok mate, look forward to it."

"Of course Saron is invited, or whoever is flavour of the month, John."

"Ha-ha, funny guy, hey?"

It was almost 11.55pm when John called it a night and headed back to his cottage. He wasn't sure about Imogen but if Steve was happy that's all that mattered.

The following morning John headed for work but called first at Beryl's Baps for a doorstep bacon sandwich and a mug of strong black coffee. While he was eating his sandwich his phone rang. It was Anouska.

"Anouska, what are you playing at?"

"John, I am sorry. I came over and stayed with a girl I knew, but her husband was a drug dealer. During that night men came and emptied the flat. I panicked and went home with Anka. I am not a bad person John. I wanted you to see your daughter."

Anouska then got upset.

"Hey, don't cry, it's ok. It was just a shock that's all."

"So, you are not mad with me, John?"

"No, everything is fine."

"Look John, I have to go. Anka is crawling everywhere."

"Ok Anouska, anytime, call me," and the phone went dead.

Why was his life so complicated he thought? With his breakfast and drink finished he headed into Bixton.

"Good morning Magic, get all the officers in the incident room and forensics please."

"Will do, Sir."

John quickly nipped to his office and hung his coat up before taking a quick look at his post and the paperwork that was building up like some kind of torture for him.

The incident room was full when John arrived.

"Ok everybody, as you are aware we still have the Helen Spirios murder and our colleague Sandra and no clues. Now we have the murder of one Amy Lord. Her husband Cuthbert Lord found her stabbed to death in bed. Hopefully Wally has got some DNA to help us out with this."

Wally stood up.

"The woman had been stabbed through the heart in the house. We found a scribbled piece of paper which simply said, 'none believer'. We did find two hairs and we did manage to get DNA from them, but this hasn't matched to anybody on the data base at the moment."

"Keep looking Wally, this could be a massive breakthrough."

Wally went back and sat down.

"So, this may not be a bad one to solve with Wally's help. I want resources throwing at Sandra's murderer, everybody. DI Smarty you take charge of this with DI Lee, DI Milton and DS Bass. DI Kiernan you will be working with me on the current case. Thanks everyone."

Gammon pulled DI Kiernan aside.

"Been quite impressed with you lad, and we have a permanent position here at Bixton which I would like to offer you."

"I don't know what to say, Sir."

"Well, yes might be a good start, lad. "Then yes it is, Sir."

"Welcome aboard."

"Right I want you to do some digging on Cuthbert Lord and Tommy Spire. You know bank accounts, previous convictions. Firstly we need to go to Lingcliffe, Pippa's Frozen Foods for a chat with lover boy."

They were just about to leave when Wally came rushing over.

"John, on the base of the victim's foot there are three letters, 'RPF'."

"What do you mean?"

"Just that John, three letters 'RPF', actually carved in her right foot."

"Ok thanks, Wally."

PAY FOR YOUR SIN

Gammon and Kiernan set off for Lingcliffe.

"Bit odd that, Sir. Why RPF?"

"I can't imagine our killer is stupid enough to mark the victim's body with his or her initials, so we have to assume it means something else, Danny."

"I agree Sir, but it's a bit bizarre to say the least."

Gammon and Kiernan entered the reception area of Pippa's Frozen Foods. The young lady at the front desk pleasantly smiled.

"How may I help you?"

"I'm DCI Gammon and this is DI Kiernan," Gammon said showing his warrant card.

"Could we have a word with a Mr Tommy Spire?"

"I'm afraid he is out to lunch with customers, but should be back shortly."

"Ok, we will wait here."

The reception area was nicely set up with a large sixty five inch flat screen TV showing the factories facilities. Almost twenty minutes passed before four men in suits arrived. The young girl on reception beckoned the man in a blue suit and flash tie, then pointed to Gammon and Kiernan. Spire walked over. He reminded John of an over bearing car salesman with his thick blonde hair, pearly white teeth and dapper dress sense.

"Mr Spire, I wondered if we could have a word?"

"Well, it's a little inconvenient."

"Well, we could discuss this at the station if you would prefer?"

"Just a minute, Mr Gammon."

He went back to the party and Gammon heard him make an excuse that some other customers had arrived, so he would have to cut short their meeting.

Spire then returned and told the young girl to make coffee and to bring it through to his office. This was some plush office, the carpets felt like you were sinking in quick sand they were so deep. He had three big TV's on the walls and a large state of the art desk with a laptop.

The young girl brought the coffee in with a small glass dish with home-made chocolates.

"Thank you Kylie, that will be all."

Spire poured the coffees; black for Gammon, white no sugar for Kiernan.

"Help yourselves to the chocolates gentlemen."

He hadn't got the words out of his mouth before Kiernan was filling his face.

"Mr Spire, we are led to believe that you are, or sorry you were, in a relationship with Mrs Amy Lord," and Gammon emphasised the 'Mrs'.

"What do you mean were?"

"I'm afraid she was found murdered yesterday."

"No, really, poor lady."

"So, you did know her then, Mr Spire."

"Only slightly, Mr Gammon."

"Were you lovers, Mr Spire?"

"If you mean had we slept together? Then yes, one night after a party at the Star in Puddle Dale. We hit it off, and I'm a single man, so why not? That isn't a crime, is it Mr Gammon?"

"Well, I'm not sure Mr Lord would think it wasn't, Mr Spire."

"That's his choice, if he can't satisfy his wife, not my problem."

"Ok, where were you last night between the hours of 8.00am and 9.15am yesterday morning, Mr Spire?"

PAY FOR YOUR SIN

"I was here at work. I am working on a big presentation for a frozen food company we are hoping to supply on the West Coast of America."

"Could anyone vouch for you, Mr Spire?"

"I didn't see anybody, Mr Gammon."

"So, we only have your word for that then?"

"Yes, I guess so."

DI Kiernan got up and started looking at some awards on the wall which Gammon thought was odd.

"What does RPF stand for, Mr Spire?"

"Real Perfection Fish. Why?"

"Oh, just wondered."

"Who are Real Perfection Fish?"

"It's just a marketing name for our frozen fish products in America."

"Mr Spire, I would like you to pop into the station tomorrow to have a DNA test."

"Why?"

"Well I have reason to believe that hair found on the victim's body could have your DNA on it. Now will you cooperate please, Mr Spire?"

"Ok, not a problem, I have done nothing wrong I can assure you."

"Ok, report to Bixton Police Station and ask for DI Daniel Kiernan. Mr Spire, we won't keep you any longer. I'm sure you have plenty to do we will see ourselves out."

Gammon and Kiernan thanked the young girl and left Pippa's Frozen Foods and headed back to Bixton.

"Do you think it's him, Sir?"

"I don't know to be honest Danny. He seemed ok with giving a DNA sample, unless he is over confident."

"What about the RPF reference in his office?"

PAY FOR YOUR SIN

"It could have been a coincidence, but we will see."

When they arrived back at Bixton it was almost 4.00pm so Gammon told DI Kiernan to finish the shift off looking into Tommy Spire. He decided to wade through the paperwork that was staring at him from his desk. Gammon didn't leave until 6.00pm hoping the next day DI Smarty might have a lead on Sandra's killer.

There was only one place he was heading for, that was the Spinning Jenny. The bar area was in full flow which surprised John. Carol Lestar was a bit the worse for wear, she was dancing with Jimmy Lowcee. John fought his way to the bar.

"Flippin' heck Kev, what's going off?"

"It's been Eric Smalley's funeral out of the village. He always said when he was gone he wanted a disco at his wake and loads of colour, so Carol organised it."

"I didn't know he had passed away mate."

"About a week ago. He had gone racing at Uttoxeter, won one hundred and forty quid on the last race, and had a massive heart attack going to collect his winnings."

"Hey, me and Doreen have had an invite to Steve and Imogen's wedding."

"Blimey that was quick, he only asked me to be his best man yesterday."

"Imogen delivered them by hand, so I am guessing yours will be at your cottage. She said you were to be Steve's best man, mate."

"You look unsure, John?"

PAY FOR YOUR SIN

"Just hope he isn't on the rebound, Kev. You know Steve, always dives in and bugger the consequences."

"Well, I don't think you will ever change him, John."

"Guess not, Kev. Give me a pint of bitter mate, and one for you."

The pub was heaving. John knew quite a few, but they were mainly from an older age group, so he just had two pints and decided to call it a night.

He was almost home when his mobile rang.

"Sir, it's DI Lee. I am at Puddle Dale sheltered accommodation, there has been a murder."

"Ok Peter, I'm on my way. Have you got forensics on the case?"

"Yes Sir, and DI Milton is here."

"Ok Peter, on my way."

It was lucky he had had just the two pints he thought as he headed to Puddle Dale.

Gammon arrived and there was a good police presence. DI Lee met him.

"Wally is in the flat, Sir and I have just spoken to the warden who found the body. She is over here, Sir."

The lady looked quite distressed.

"Hello, I'm DCI Gammon and you are?"

"Margaret Staffy, I'm the warden here, Mr Gammon."

"Ok Margaret, I realise this is upsetting but anything you can remember will help us."

DI Lee took notes.

"Well I always go to see Annie about 4.30pm every day."

"What was Annie's surname, please Margaret?"

"Oh sorry, Board, Annie Board."

PAY FOR YOUR SIN

"How old was she?"

"She would have been eighty next week."

"Did Annie seem distressed about anything?"

"No, quite the opposite, she had been laughing with me. Although a couple of days earlier a man came who said his name was Dick.

"Did he say what his business was or give a surname?"

"No, and I asked Annie if she was ok after he left. She seemed upset, but she said she was alright and I didn't like to pry."

"Dick, do you know where he was from?"

"No, I'm sorry I don't."

"Could you give a description to my officer, Margaret?"

"Yes, I think so."

"Did he have a car?"

"Yes, it was blue."

"Would you know the make?"

"No, I'm sorry."

"So, you saw her at 4.30pm, and you left at what time?"

"4.45pm. I have to get round them all you see, so Annie used to call our fifteen minutes the witching hour."

"So, you came back at what time?"

"It would have been 6.00pm. I shouldn't go back again, but I liked Annie and I always said goodnight to her. She would always have a nip of whisky before she got in bed."

"Just run through what you found when you went in Annie's flat."

"Well, I tried the door because sometimes Annie would lock it, but she hadn't so I went in. I called to her but there was no answer. I could hear the telly on in the bedroom, so I poured her a small whisky and took it through to her like I had many times before."

"I'm afraid I dropped the glass when I saw her throat had been cut and there was blood everywhere. I screamed and ran out. Mr Potts met me on the hallway as he had heard me scream and he called for an ambulance and the Police."

"Ok Margaret, I think we have enough now. If you would give my Detective Inspector a description of the man that came to see Annie, and if I need any more help I will be in touch. Thank you."

Gammon wandered towards the bedroom. He put his head round the door much to the annoyance of Wally.

"Get out John, you will contaminate the murder scene."

"Come on then Wally, what have you got for me?"

"Very little at the moment, other than under right foot the killer carved into the sole of her foot 'RPF'."

"Bloody hell Wally, what is this all about?"

"Not got a clue John, but whoever is doing this is a nut case mate."

"Ok, can we have a meeting in the morning, say 9.00am?"

"Yes, should have something for you by then, mate."

The following morning Gammon assembled everyone in the incident room and put up a picture of Annie Board.

"Ok everyone, this is our latest victim. The person or persons are not hanging about, that's two now. We have victim one Amy Lord, and victim two," he said pointing at Annie Board.

PAY FOR YOUR SIN

"Both victims had 'RPF' carved into the sole of their right foot. Both had the words 'Non Believer' written on the wall."

"Yesterday myself and DI Kiernan interviewed Tommy Spire the Marketing Director at Pippa's Frozen Foods. Spire admitted he was Amy Lords lover, and DI Kiernan also spotted on the wall of his office the words 'RPF'. He said it stood for 'Real Perfection Fish' which is a marketing strategy for the West Coast of America."

"Wally, have you anything for us?"

Wally stood up.

"On the wall were the words 'None Believer', the same as the first victim. We also had DNA from hair strands found on the victim which matched the first victim's assailant. We have yet to find a match on the DNA data base."

"Yes, DI Milton."

"What about Tommy Spire? Has he had his DNA taken?"

"Yes, he is coming in this morning to see DI Kiernan."

"There is a fair possibility that the killer of the first victim also killed the second, and hopefully he or she are careless. Hopefully we will know more after Spire has been tested."

"Right, the rest of the team, what have we on Helen Spirios and Sandra's murders?"

"Yes, DI Lee."

"Right Sir, we have that all makes of van that are green or grey. There are twenty seven green Transits in the Peak District and eleven grey ones. DI Milton and DI Smarty checked them out, so I will hand you over to DI Smarty."

"We found three which were total wrecks, twenty one that could all stipulate where they or their vans were on the night of Sandra's abduction. The other three vans are owned by a William Marks who runs a bread delivery service. He said all three vans were in his yard that night, as he delivers about 4.00 am. His two employees each had alibis and Mark's wife also backed him up that all three vans were not out that night."

"Of the eleven grey ones, ten were owned by a company called Quick Deliver. All vans were out that night, all tachographs checked out, and also each van has a tracker. None were in the vicinity of Alford in the Water so we can count those out. That left just one van to find. Thanks to some sterling work by DS Winnipeg, the van was registered to an Arthur Mann of Rowksly. We went to the house but it was empty. DS Winnipeg you take over."

"The house was a terraced house with a gravel pull in round the back. The grey van was in the pull-in. The next door neighbour came to see who I was, and I explained I was looking for an Arthur Mann at this address. She said the house was owned by Mr Spirios from the chip shop in the village."

There was a gasp in the room as the realisation that DS Winnipeg had possibly solved the murders.

"Right DI Milton, get the van brought back to the yard. Wally, I want full sweep of this van. DI Lee and DS Bass go and arrest Dimitri Spirios and bring him in for questioning. He will need a solicitor and keep him overnight. I will question him in the morning after our meeting."

"DI Smarty, you and DS Winnipeg get a warrant for the house where the van is parked, and I want it going over with a fine-tooth comb."

"Thanks everyone. Great work, DS Winnipeg. DI Kiernan, let me know when the DNA result is through from Wally. Don't let Tommy Spire go anywhere until we have the result."

"Ok, Sir."

"I will be in my office Danny, I have a lot of calls to make."

Gammon went back to his office, his stomach churning, this could be a momentous day if we get two killers on the same day he thought.

It was time to get Chief Constable Sim up to speed. Sim could not have been happier.

"Well done John, let's keep our fingers crossed. I don't want to count my chickens before they have hatched, but I think we maybe on a winner."

Gammon hung up and read some of the report DI Kiernan had placed on his desk about Tommy Spire. Spire had been divorced three years earlier and had a massive divorce settlement. That's how he bought into the business at Lingcliffe.

It stated that Spire was forty two years old. At eighteen he was sent to prison for beating a woman within an inch of her life. He got eleven years and was out in eight. His bank accounts appeared clean, nothing untoward.

Gammon was starting to feel he had his man. It was almost 4.00pm when Kiernan knocked on Gammon's door.

"We've got him, Sir. The DNA on the two bodies match exactly to Tommy Spire."

"Great, well done Danny. Go down and tell him to get a solicitor."

"He brought one with him, Sir."

PAY FOR YOUR SIN

"Even better, let's sort this."

DI Kiernan set the tape going.

"DCI Gammon, DI Kiernan, Tommy Spire," Gammon said and "Walter Scribe," the solicitor added.

"Mr Spire."

"Please call me Tommy."

"Ok Tommy, we have DNA from two bodies that were murdered by the same person and it matches your sample given today."

"I'm sorry Mr Gammon, are you saying I am a murderer?"

"It is certainly looking that way, Tommy. Why would hair from you be on both victim's bodies, Amy Lord and Alice Board?"

"I seriously don't know, Mr Gammon. I told you that I had slept with Amy, but I didn't know this other woman, Alice? I really don't know how this could happen."

"Are you a violent man, Tommy?"

"I would say not, Mr Gammon."

"You see Mr Spire, that's where we disagree. You were arrested and imprisoned for beating a woman within an inch of her life, to which you spent eight years in Leicester prison."

At this Tommy Spire became aggressive.

"Look, I have turned my life round. I was a young foolish person back then, I am not that person anymore."

"Tommy, do you know I almost believe you, but you have to admit you have been violent towards women. Each woman had 'RPF' carved into their right foot. My DI spotted your little marketing logo, and guess what that said? 'RPF', not very clever, Tommy."

Gammon pushed the times of the murders in front of Spire and his solicitor.

PAY FOR YOUR SIN

"Can you tell me where you were at these times, Tommy?"

"Amy Lord, I was at work early that day."

"Can anybody vouch for you on that?"

"I'm not sure, I didn't go into the factory."

"Well surely Tommy, with the seriousness of the allegations we are discussing, you would know if you were talking to anybody? Just maybe a hello in passing?"

Spire thought for a moment.

"No, I don't think I saw anybody."

"Ok we move on, what about Annie Board? Were you in Puddle Dale on the night of the murder of Annie Board, Tommy?"

"Well I had been in the Star Inn all afternoon."

"What time did you leave?"

"I think it was about 4.30pm or maybe 5.00pm."

At this point Gammon had heard enough.

"Tommy Spire, I am arresting you for the murders of Amy Lord and Annie Board. You don't have to say anything but anything you do say maybe taken down and used in evidence against you. Do you understand?"

"This is bloody prosperous. I am due to go to America in the morning to launch our frozen food range."

"You won't be going anywhere."

"Take him to the holding cell please."

Spire was protesting his innocence, but Gammon was sure it all pointed to Spire.

Back at his office he went through the case with Chief Constable Sim who was over the moon at the result, and the thought they may have a lead on Sandra's murderer.

Everything was falling into place, but he just hoped the rest of the team came good on Helen Spirios and Sandra's murders.

Gammon left quite late so decided to ask Doreen for a take-away as he couldn't be bothered cooking. There was only Phil Sterndale with Sheba Filey and Carol Lestar and Jimmy Lowcee in the corner. Kev was behind the bar.

"What you drinking, John?" asked Phil Sterndale.

"I'll have a Pedigree, thanks. How are you two?"

"Good thanks John. We are going to HaWez tomorrow to the sheep sales with Stephen Condray and his new girl Fiona Scott."

"Oh Steve, he is a nice lad. His parents have farmed next to my parents for I bet forty odd years. Where is the new girlfriend from?"

"Biffin, near Hittington."

"Not a name I know mate."

"No, she only moved into Biffin Grange with her parents about eight months ago. Oh, and Jim and Lisa Tink are coming. Lisa wants a few sheep apparently."

"Sounds like a good day."

"Oh no mate we are going for three nights. Will be a proper session," and Phil laughed.

"We are going to look at sheep Philip."

"I know my dear, only joking," and he winked at John.

"My grandad won best of sheep twelve years running, John and has a plaque at the market with his name on it."

"I bet you are proud of that, Sheba?"

PAY FOR YOUR SIN

"Immensely, John."

"Kev, another round of drinks, and can I order the lasagne with garlic bread and salad to take out, mate?"

"It will be half an hour, mate."

"That's fine, Kev."

The Sandra murder was playing on John's mind so he wasn't feeling to chatty, and was glad when Doreen brought his take out for him.

Back home John set up the table in the garden and poured himself a large Jameson's. While he sat eating his lasagne two small squirrels were playing in the tree. John threw a piece of garlic bread about three feet in front of him to tempt the squirrels.

To John's surprise they came and took the bread, but instead of running away with it they jumped on the table and ate it while John was eating his lasagne. He loved nature and vowed that once they had got Helen Spirios and Sandra's murderer he was going to do some serious walking, an get some fresh air in his lungs.

John was at the station for 8.00am and told Magic to make sure everyone was in the incident room for a meeting at 9.00am.

Gammon sat in his office, the sun light was streaming through his office window as if a strong light was being shone from Losehill. Gammon was hoping the day could match the result from the team in the meeting.

He tackled a couple of reports then headed down to the meeting. Gammon could tell something seemed good, the room was buzzing.

"Ok everyone, I'm hoping we have some good news. Yes Wally."

PAY FOR YOUR SIN

"The grey van registered to a Mr Arthur Mann had blood from both Helen Spirios and DI Scooper. We also found hair from DI Scooper."

"Any other DNA from maybe our killer?"

"No, other than that the van had been cleaned quite thoroughly."

"Ok now, what about the Spirios house? There was of course DNA from Helen Spirios, but we found nothing to tie in with the murder of DI Scooper."

"Well as you all know I charged Tommy Spire with the murders of Amy Lord and Annie Board, so I think we have that one in the bag. I will now interview Spirios with DS Bass who will do the recording, and DI Smarty will interview with me. I am pretty sure Spirios knows more than he is letting on. If we crack this the beers are on me tonight."

Gammon entered the interview room. He introduced everyone including Arran Bilscombe the solicitor.

"Ok Mr Spirios, am I ok to call you Dimitri?"

"Yes, it is not a problem everybody know Dimitri."

"So, Dimitri we went to number eleven Rowksly Hill Road, a house I believe you own. Is that correct?"

"Yes, I buy house so one day my brother he come to live in Rowksly."

"At the property we discovered a grey van registered to a Mr Arthur Mann."

Dimitri looked shocked.

"Is Arthur Mann you, Dimitri?"

"No, I don't know Arthur Mann."

"Have you ever rented the house to anyone?"

"Will I be in trouble?"

"Why?"

PAY FOR YOUR SIN

"I rent house for cash to Polish workers."

"So, do you keep an inventory who you have rented the house to?"

"No, my Helen she does this. I fry fish, that is my job."

"Dimitri, I am unsure you are telling us the truth. You need to, this is very serious. We have found blood from your wife and blood and hair from DI Scooper in the back of the grey van registered to Arthur Mann, so I suggest you get your thinking hat on, Dimitri."

"My wife she use the van, so maybe she cut herself."

"So, you know about the van?"

"Only that my wife borrow sometimes from man who live there."

"And was that man called Arthur Mann?"

"I tell you I don't know, I never meet him."

Dimitri spoke to his solicitor with his hand cupped to his mouth.

"I remember, I meet him maybe two times."

"Can you give us a description?"

"He had grey hair and my height."

"So, five feet ten, Dimitri?"

"Yes, I think so."

"Well let me tell you what I think. I think this Arthur Mann was having an affair with your wife and you found out, so you killed her and this Arthur Mann. And I think Sandra Scooper had rumbled you. Am I on the right track?"

Suddenly Dimitri broke down and started to cry. He could hardly get his words out.

"I loved my wife, but she liked other men. I found out she was seeing this Arthur Mann who was living in our house. I went to the house and caught them in bed. I hit him with candle stick holder and then I hit her the same."

"I thought I had killed them, so I bundled them into grey van. I was very upset Mr Gammon. I loved Helen. Anyway I decided to bury them on a moor. I set off, but it was raining so heavy something must have got wet and the van cut out in Alford on Water."

"What then? Did DI Scooper stop to help you?"

"Yes, I told I was ok, but she insisted and opened the back of the van. Mann was coming round so I hit her and him again. This time I killed Mann and Helen. DI Scooper was still alive. I took her onto Micklock Moor to help me bury the bodies. I locked her in the shed while I dug two graves."

"I didn't want to kill her but when I got back into the shed she had worked her way free. She put up big fight like wild cat, but I killed her. I went to bury the other two, but it was raining so hard the graves had filled up with water. I had read about the serial killer and the body parts. I did the same, so you would be looking for the serial killer. Arthur Mann, I fed to my pigs, they enjoyed him. That man, he caused all this, I am bad man and so sorry."

"Dimitri Spirios, I am charging you with the murders of DI Sandra Scooper, Helen Spirios and Arthur Mann."

Gammon carried on reading Spirios his rights while he blubbered like a child.

Gammon felt physically sick at what happened to Sandra and for days couldn't sleep. With all the murders now put to bed Chief Constable threw a wake in honour of Sandra and as a thank you for the hard work the team had put into solving these

PAY FOR YOUR SIN

murders, and the 'RPF' murders as they were called by the press.

CHAPTER TWO

A few months passed Dimitri Spirios had been given two life term sentences for the murder of his wife and Sandra Scooper. He also received twelve years for the disappearance of Arthur Mann who was never found.

Tommy Spire received two life sentences for the murders of Annie Board and Amy Lord. Throughout the trial he protested his innocence, but the jury were having none of it. At the summing up Judge Isles said Tommy Spire was a danger to women, quite possibly a psychopath, with a total disregard for human life. He was oblivious to his crimes, actually believing he didn't do these terrible things.

Judge Isles said Spire would be assessed for his mental state, but that life must

56

mean life, with no parole to be considered for thirty five years.

John needed to call at the Spinning Jenny to see Kev, Jack, Bob and the rest of them to let them know about Steve's stag day on Saturday.

John arrived, and the pub was full of all his and Steve's friends. It was perfect, he could sort the stag day all at one go.

The weather was becoming more unsettled and Jack Etchings said the Peak District was in for one hell of a winter. The talk in the Spinning Jenny was all about Steve and Imogen's wedding, but Doreen said a strange thing.

"Because it looks like Christmas before we retire, I decided to nip to St Peter's Church at Hittington to tidy my dad's grave, and honestly you would not believe this. I finished my dad's grave and thought

I would have a coffee and a piece of cake at that little café called The Clock Strikes Three."

"Bloody hell Doreen, this is a long story."

"No longer than your dumb jokes, Bob," and they all laughed.

"Anyway, ordered my coffee and cake and sat looking round as you do, and I swear to you if I hadn't had known better but sitting in the window was Jo."

"What, Steve's Jo?"

"Well obviously it wasn't, but she was her double. I had to go over to get a better look. We struck up a conversation and I could feel a chill down my back as I talked to her.

"Hi, I'm Doreen Markham. landlady at the Spinning Jenny at Swinster. You look so much like a friend of mine."

"Oh, who is that?"

PAY FOR YOUR SIN

"Jo Wickets, that was?"

"Was?"

"Yes, I'm afraid she died some time back."

I could see she looked shocked.

"Aagh, maybe you were imagining it, with this lady looking like Jo, Doreen."

"I don't know, but what I do know is there is something strange about all this."

"Did she say where she was from?"

"She said she was from London, and she was a writer."

"What sort of books?"

"All genres, Shelley. She said her latest one was called My Lost Sister which spooked me even more."

"Are you sure you haven't dreamt this, Doreen?"

"No Jack, you ask my Kevin. I told him about it as soon as I got back."

"What did she say her name was?"

"India Green."

"Wow, what a lovely name, Doreen."

"Yeah, she was a lovely girl. I told her to call and have a drink with us as she had only just moved to the area and was renting a cottage in Hittington while she wrote her book."

"Well if we aren't in when she calls let us know, Doreen."

"I will, Cheryl."

"What about Steve? I think everybody has forgotten his feelings."

"No John, I understand, and he is marrying Imogen.

"Yes, I suppose so."

John didn't want it getting back to Steve that he felt negative towards Imogen.

"Anyway, let's get off the subject are you still on for Steve's stag party?"

Jack, Bob, Kev and Phil all said, "Yes but what are we doing?"

PAY FOR YOUR SIN

"Well I thought a pub crawl. Start at the Wobbly Man in Toad Holes then Wop and Take at Trissington, onto Tow'd Man, then The Limping Duck. Then call at the Sycamore at Pritwich to see Tony and Rita, as he is too busy to get away, then end up here at The Spinning Jenny. Would you do us a curry, Doreen?"

"Not a problem, love. Tell me how many for and I will do a Chilli Curry and some Bhajis etc."

"That would be great. We will be ready for something to eat. I thought this Saturday lads, starting at Wobbly for 12.30pm."

"I'll drive you about. John. My lad's got a twelve seater mini bus so I don't mind."

"Are you sure Shelley?"

"Yes, not a problem. I can keep my eye on Jack then," and she laughed.

Jack gave her that look of disagreement.

"Do you want picking up from home you lot, or give me a call when you have finished at the Wobbly?"

"We will give you a call after the Wobbly Man, Shelley, thank you very much."

"What's happening with the new people and the pub then, Doreen?"

"Well, it's between two couples; Jimmy Lowcee and Carol Lestar, and Wez and Lyndsay Villa."

"Where are they from?"

"Barnsley, and to be honest I think they will probably clinch the deal the way it is going. They have some big plans for the place."

"Will you be doing anything with whoever gets it?"

"Well I have offered if they are struggling, but to be honest me and Kev are looking forward to retirement, Bob."

PAY FOR YOUR SIN

"Ok everybody, I'm off."

"Bloody hell, John Gammon first one to leave. Are you on a promise lad?"

"No, nothing like that Jack, just need to get in early tomorrow got a mountain of paperwork since the promotion."

"Ok lad, goodnight."

John was pleased he had the stag day sorted so he quickly phoned Steve, but thought better of mentioning the Jo lookalike.

The following day Gammon mentioned to DI Lee, Smarty and Milton about the stag day on Saturday. Only DI Lee said he couldn't make it as he was taking the grandchildren to see Disney on Ice in Nottingham.

Things were reasonably quiet at the station, other than a couple of house break ins, and a domestic fall out which

Gammon sent DS Bass to cut her teeth on being her first domestic.

Gammon still detested the mountain of daily paperwork, but at least Chief Constable Sim was happy with the way Bixton was being run.

It was the day of Steve's stag do and Tracey Rodgers said she would drop Steve, John, Jack and Bob at the Wobbly Man.

Steve was full of excitement, but John couldn't get what Doreen had said out of his mind. With the first lot of drinks bought. John stood talking to Jack Etchings. It wasn't long before Bob couldn't contain himself.

"Hey Steve, Doreen was telling us last night how she had seen your Jo's double in a coffee shop in Hittington."

John dived in quick.

PAY FOR YOUR SIN

"There will only be one Jo, hey Steve. Leave the guy alone Bob, let him enjoy his stag party."

Kev was furious with Bob and waited for him to go to the toilet and gave him a piece of his mind.

"Trouble with you Bob, you think everything in life is like one of your jokes. It isn't, that could have ruined Steve's day if John hadn't dived in.

"Sorry Kev, I didn't think."

"That's the problem, you don't bloody think."

"I will go and apologise."

"No you don't, leave it now, and let's hope Steve has brushed it off."

Rick Hieb, landlord at the Wobbly Man, got a round in for the stag party.

"Very good of you, Rick."

"Hey, got to look after a fellow landlord, Steve."

"Oh yeah, I suppose I am."

One more drink then it was time to go to the next pub on the crawl.

"Hey, why don't we try that pub that just re-opened?"

"What George and Dragon, Steve?"

"Yeah, flippin' heck, that must have been shut all of seventeen years."

"Yeah, two blokes took it on and they have refurbed it and got a micro-brewery in the old stables. They call it The Chicken Foot Tap House mate."

"Sounds good to me."

Kev started herding everybody out of the Wobbly Man to walk three hundred yards down the village to The Chicken Foot Tap House, as only Kev could. Jimmy Lowcee had got drinking chasers with Dave Smarty. Smarty had a bit of a wobble on as they walked to Chicken Foot.

PAY FOR YOUR SIN

The pub had changed beyond recognition. All the tables were rustic. They had five Chicken Foot brews on tap with pork pies, pickled eggs and ploughman's the order of the day.

"What can I get you chaps?" the girl behind the bar remarked.

"Aren't you Katrina Salford?"

"Yes, well not quite correct. I just got married to Mick Dome one of the owners. Do I know you?"

"Yes, we went to Toad Holes Junior School until you were about nine if I remember. I'm Carl Milton."

"Blimey Carl Milton, you were that annoying little boy that used to pull my hair in class."

All the lads cheered.

"Always been useless with women, Milton," shouted Jimmy Lowcee.

"Oh, listen Mr Gigolo himself, now he is seeing Carol Lestar."

"Rowdy lot, aren't they Mr Gammon?"

"How do you know my name?"

Katrina Dome was about five feet nine and well-dressed. John always noticed shoes and they weren't Clarks he thought. She had long dark hair and looked like one of those beauties out of a Gypsy film he thought.

"Everybody knows John Gammon, you are always on the telly."

"All for the wrong reasons Katrina, I'm afraid. So what beer do you recommend?"

"Well this one is Hen Race and it's an amber beer, 3.9%. This one is called Cockerel again Amber beer 4.4%. Then we have Chicken Shack 4.8% a hoppy beer, Furry Foot 5.1% a dark beer and finally Rooster Black Cock which is 9.2% more like a porter ale."

PAY FOR YOUR SIN

"That's it then, thirteen Rooster Black Cocks please Katrina."

The beer flowed.

"Bloody hell, John. I'm feeling the pace a bit."

"Come on Smarty, you having a chaser with it."

"No, was just telling John, I best slow up a bit."

Jimmy laughed as he downed his chaser with little or no effect.

"Look John, they have groups on Friday and Saturday nights. Do you think I should tell Katrina I'm a comedian?"

"I reckon she has probably worked that one out for herself, mate."

"Right everybody, I have a mini bus outside to take us to the Wop and Take in Trissington so sup up."

A great amount of cheers followed. John and Steve thanked Katrina and they followed the mob to the mini bus.

The Wop and Take was a lovely pub owned by Saron's family and had some great memories for John.

"My shout."

"About time, Kev."

"Hey, I never miss my round, Mr Etchings."

"I'm only joking you silly old buggar."

Kev ordered thirteen double brandies. One or two were struggling. Smarty kept nipping to the toilets, it was anyone's guess why. Jimmy Lowcee was in full flow. Looking round, John could only see maybe him, Kev, Steve and Carl going the full course. Two more rounds of the same and the mini bus was waiting.

"Tow'd Man, here we come."

PAY FOR YOUR SIN

John nipped to the toilet. He wanted to look presentable in case Saron was working. Luckily the Tow'd Man was quiet. Saron was behind the bar. Jimmy Lowcee ordered thirteen Slippery Nipples, a concoction of Baileys and Sambuca.

"There you go lads, down in one."

Smarty finished his and ran outside to be sick. Saron arranged a taxi home for him and Bob, who also was on the point of collapse.

"Bloody light-weights. Now where?"

"Well, we were going to the Limping Duck, but think we best miss that one and go and see Tony and Rita at The Sycamore in Pritwich."

They all agreed so headed for the Sycamore. Tony was behind the bar and he called Rita to tell her Steve, Jack and John were here.

Rita came out and was so pleased to see them she hugged John then Steve then Jack.

"Where's Bob?"

"He went home after the Tow'd Man."

"Oh blimey, Cheryl isn't going to be very pleased, Jack."

"We know," and they laughed in unison.

"Tony get them all a drink."

"It's my round."

"No we insist, Jack. You order what they want."

"Thanks Rita. Can we have eleven Flaming Sambucas please?"

"Coming up."

"Do you reckon you could still beat me at arm wrestling, Tony?"

"Easy, Mr Lowcee."

"Ok, let's have a fiver on it."

"You will lose your money, Jimmy."

PAY FOR YOUR SIN

"No I won't John, he has been in the pub game too long now, he will have gone soft."

They cleared a table and Milton was telling Jack that he was good at arm wrestling. It didn't take Tony long to pick up the fiver from Jimmy Lowcee, laughing but with ego bruised.

"Can I have a go, Tony?"

"If you want lad."

Carl stepped forward like a scene out of a darts final. They were all shouting, "Tony, Tony."

Tony again mad light work of poor Carl and picked up another fiver. Steve couldn't resist the challenge.

"I'm next," he shouted.

Steve had powerful arms, so Tony was a bit tactical. Twice they both came close to winning before Tony had one last push, beating Steve to pick up the fiver.

"Come on John, you have to have a go."

John declined but they persisted.

"Well if Steve can't beat him, I have no chance."

He wasn't far wrong, it took Tony less than thirty seconds to claim another fiver.

"Right you lot, time for the Spinning Jenny, not that you lot will be able to drink much more."

"We'll see."

"Kev wasn't counting you, Jimmy."

They said their goodbyes and climbed into the mini bus and headed for their final destination, The Spinning Jenny.

Once inside Doreen asked John what time he wanted the food putting out.

"Can I say about an hour please?"

"Not a problem, chicken," she said as she headed back to the kitchen while carol Lestar served them. Joni was also working.

PAY FOR YOUR SIN

Steve and John were deep in conversation when Jack told John he wanted him. Thinking Jack must be feeling poorly he pulled him aside.

"What's up mate?"

"Take a look in that corner?"

"Where?"

"There John."

John couldn't believe his eyes. It was Jo's double.

"I'm going over to have a word, mate. Keep Steve busy."

"Will do, John."

"Hi, I'm John. Are you Doreen's friend, India?"

"Yes, did she tell you about me?"

"Only that you had met, and you might pop in for a drink."

"Where are you from, India?"

It was really uncanny. She was Jo's double, she even sounded like her.

"I'm from London originally, but I am doing my family tree in between writing my latest book."

"Oh, you are an author, are you?"

"Yes, you can count that amongst my many sins."

"Did your family live up this way?"

"Well, if the genealogists are to be believed she had a farm, but most of it is gone now due to a fire apparently."

John felt a cold shiver run down his back.

"Is that connection the end of the Derbyshire connection?"

"I don't know, I'm still looking. I was adopted as a baby and until my adopted parents died I never knew. They never told me. But why should they I guess? Only thing I remember was when I was about seven my adopted mother's sister said I looked like my identical twin. I asked her about it, but she said she had been joking. There could not be two of me, as they had thrown the mould away when I was born!"

John's detective skills knew this was Jo's sister but what was he going to do?

"Look, really enjoyed your company but my publisher is on my case for the book, so I best get back and do some work. See you again," and she left.

She walked like Jo talked like Jo and even laughed like Jo. The only thing slightly different was she was about an inch taller than Jo.

John got back to the party.

"Who you been chatting up, mate?"

"Nobody Jimmy, just an old work colleague."

"If you believe that Jimmy, you will believe anything. Only saw her from the back but she was a stunner, Steve."

"Ok lads, you have had your fun. What are we drinking next?"

"Very good of you Carl, what about eleven blackcurrant Sambucas?"

"Sounds good to me Steve."

"Are you going to get Doreen to put the food out, Kev?"

"I'll go Kev," he said in a slurred reply.

Only Doreen was in the kitchen, so John told her what he had found out about India.

"I told you, John."

"The thing is Doreen, he is marrying Imogen in a week."

"So why would that matter, John?"

"Well you have seen India. She is Jo's double, it will freak him out. I shouldn't say this, but between us I think he is on the rebound from Jo. You know how Steve is, he would never admit it, would he?"

PAY FOR YOUR SIN

"You know him better than me John, talk to him."

"Yeah you are right, I will."

John didn't go into detail about India being adopted just in case it was all just a coincidence.

Doreen brought out rice, chilli curry, beef curry, baby roast potatoes and pigs in blankets.

"Done us proud there you have, Doreen."

"Always do, don't I?"

"Best cook in the Peak District, eh Kev?"

"Well I think so Steve, but I'm biased," and he laughed.

John decided to see if Steve would go for a beer in Trissington on the Sunday on the pretence it was a hair of the dog thing, but he needed to tell him about India.

The night slowly fizzled out just leaving Carl Milton asleep in the window, Steve falling asleep on the bar and Kev and John chatting over a brandy.

"Right you lot, carry Carl out and get yourselves in my car and I will take you all home."

"Thanks, Doreen."

"Roll on retirement, then you lot can bloody walk."

"You love looking after us."

"Less of your cheek Lineman, or you will be bloody walking," and she laughed. The lads helped Milton into his flat then dropped John off and finally Steve.

John quite surprised himself the following morning. He didn't feel too bad so a drink with Steve wasn't going to be a problem. Steve had said he would pick him up at 12.30pm, so he did a few jobs round the house. Then he grabbed a coffee and read his latest book 'I Am Fawn Jones', a book Shelley had recommended. It was without doubt thought-provoking. He felt he couldn't put it down and was soon at the two hundred pages mark. Best get ready it's almost 11.50am and he will be here soon he thought.

Steve arrived promptly.

"How are you, Mr Gammon?"

"Good mate, you?"

"Yeah, but I bet Bob and Carl are rough," and they both laughed.

John felt a bit apprehensive as they entered the quaint Trissington pub. It was quite busy, mainly locals but plenty of banter from the estate workers.

Steve got the drinks and John found a table in the quieter end of the pub.

"You alright, John."

"Yes, mate."

"I know you John Gammon, and I know when something is up. What is it? Are you nervous about next week and the speech?"

"No, nothing like that mate."

"Then what is it?"

"Look, there is no easy way to tell you this, but last night I was talking to a girl that was Jo's double."

"So what, John."

"I don't just mean she resembled her, she was her double, Steve."

Steve took a drink from his glass as if to buy time before answering John.

"Look, before you say anymore Steve, let me tell you what she told me."

"She is from London, Jo was from London. She came to Derbyshire to write her latest book, but she is also researching her family tree."

"How does that concern me?"

PAY FOR YOUR SIN

"Wait for it, Steve. She had found she had an aunty so went to look at the house and it was burned down. It was yours and Jo's house. She then told me she thought she was adopted, but she doesn't know why."

"Look John, this is taking some thought to compute all this."

"I know mate, but I felt you had to know."

"Ok, so she looks like Jo, but maybe she read about what happened and is going to claim on the estate making out it was her aunt's. Have you thought about that?"

After about an hour Steve made an excuse that Imogen wanted him not to be late as they had a boules match at the Star, so needed to get back.

He dropped John off at home and left, but he was very quiet on the way back from Trissington.

The detective in John wasn't going to let this die, so he decided to go into Hittington and see if he could find where India lived. It didn't take long; a few questions in the local and he had an address. India was living in what used to Charlie Timpson's old farm house that had been renovated.

John couldn't get up with his car, so he parked at the bottom of the lane and walked up to the old cottage with its small windows and equally small oak door.

John didn't know what he was going to say or do, but he had to find out. He knocked heavily on the door three times and India finally answered. She blew John away. She had small denim shorts and a stripy sailor top which showed her ample figure off.

"Oh, hello Mr Gammon, have I done something wrong?"

PAY FOR YOUR SIN

"No, quite the opposite. I have been thinking about what you told me last night and wondered if I could help you?"

"Oh wow, that would be great. Come in and I will pour you a glass of red."

"Thank you, oh and it's John by the way."

"Coming right up, John," and she giggled.

She brought John the wine and sat next to him on the settee crossing her long legs as she got comfortable.

"So how can you help me, John?"

"Well this is going to seem weird, but my best mate married a girl called Jo Wickets. She was from London."

"Ok, well lots of people are from London."

"Jo came to live in the Peak District because she had an aunty, and this aunty left her a farm."

"I'm listening John, more wine?"

"Go on then."

John felt very relaxed in India's company. While she was getting the wine she put some music on and the open fire was crackling away. It all seemed very romantic, but this girl was his best mate's deceased wife's double. How could this be right!

John carried on his story.

"The next bit you are going to think I am nuts. My mate's dead wife was an absolute double for you."

At that India almost dropped her glass of wine.

"Do you think she was my twin, John?"

"I do actually, but she never knew or at least she never told Steve.

"Did she have any other brothers or sisters?"

PAY FOR YOUR SIN

"She had one sister, a bit younger than Jo I think. She still lives in the Lodge House which was at the bottom of the drive to the house that is no longer there."

"So, she could be my sister?"

"Well I guess so, if everything is right."

"Oh John," and she flung her arms round him and kissed him passionately. John could not help himself. He reciprocated and soon they were locked in a passionate embrace. India held his hand and took him to the bedroom. Other than Saron he had never felt such lust. She was like a rash all over John. India was very athletic and physical and teased John for almost an hour to the point where he had to take control. They made the satisfaction sound both at the same time and fell back into each other's arms, fulfilment complete. John laid thinking he had done it again, only this time he was sure if Steve saw

India he would fall for her like he had Jo Wickets. If he did, how would John explain this to him?

Obviously, India was oblivious to John's concern.

"How the hell did that happen, India?"

"I don't know, I have never done anything like that before, please believe me. If I am honest I just fancied you when you sat with me last night in the pub."

"Do you think I should speak with your friend Steve and Jo's sister?

"It would be best not to at the minute, he gets married next week, and he can be a complex character."

"Ok John, I will be guided by you."

It was almost 10.00pm when John left. They had gone downstairs and India had made a light tea. They had hardly finished that when the action started again in front of the log burner.

PAY FOR YOUR SIN

As he drove back to his cottage he was cursing himself for being so weak. Then he thought; he was single, India he assumed was single, so where was the problem? John was convincing himself.

The following morning John's thoughts on the way into work were all over the place. He arrived at Bixton to be met by Magic on the front desk.

"Sir, can you call Chief Constable Sim?"

"Ok Magic."

"He didn't sound too pleased, Sir."

"Don't worry about it Magic, he will be fine."

Gammon called Sim as soon as he got in his office. It was a real cold morning with snow forecast for that afternoon.

"Good morning Sir, cold day isn't it?"

"Not interested in that Gammon. I have just had the Micklock Mercury contact me to say they have had a letter pushed through their door saying we have convicted the wrong man for the RPF murders. The letter states why the murders were done and that the killing will go on. I am seeing Harold Costly at 2.00pm at the Limping Duck I want you there. Let's bloody hope for your sake and the force's reputation that this is a hoax."

"Ok Sir."

The phone went dead abruptly.

Gammon stood up watching the first signs of snow falling on Losehill. I couldn't have got this wrong he thought. This must be a hoax or copycat killer.

John left Bixton at 1.15pm. He wanted to make sure he was on time. Andrew Sim was already in the car park at the Limping Duck when he arrived, and he didn't look too happy.

PAY FOR YOUR SIN

"Get in the car Gammon, I want to speak with you regarding this situation. If this is true and not a copycat like you think, we have a serious problem. The media will be looking for blood. You and me are the first in the firing line."

For the first time the Chief Constable had shown his true colours. Yet again a senior office was prepared to throw Gammon under the bus to save his own career and Gammon knew it.

Gammon and Sim entered the Limping Duck. Harold Costly was sitting in a corner seat waiting smugly as he stood to shake the hand of Sim but not John's. This felt like a done deal and he was to be the fall guy.

"Mr Costly, your telephone call to me was very concerning, could I look at the letter please?"

Costly handed a copy to Sim and reluctantly one to Gammon.

John started to read.

'Mr Costly

I have chosen the Micklock Mercury to share with you that I am the real killer of Amy Lord. She was an adulteress and deserved it as she was a sinner. I broke into her home and killed her and marked her with RPF. Her stupid husband almost caught me so he is lucky he is alive, but he hadn't done anything wrong.

I then killed that silly old women in that sheltered accommodation. She was also a sinner. She had stolen from her employee twenty years ago, so she had to pay for her sins. I marked her also with RPF.

So you see Mr Costly they have the wrong man in prison and I will prove it and will kill a sinner again very soon.'

PAY FOR YOUR SIN

Sim looked at Gammon.

"This is all well and good, but anybody can write this who has followed the cases."

"So, I can say the police are not taking this seriously, can I Mr Gammon?"

"Well I think that would be foolish if only that this nut case would probably kill somebody for the hell of it. So my advice would be to do nothing Mr Costly until we have looked into this further. I will need the original letter for forensic evidence please."

Sim looked quite pleased how Gammon had handled Costly and John could sense the mood lighten somewhat.

Gammon and Sim left the Limping Duck with a crest-fallen Costly who said he would hand the original letter into the police station that afternoon. Gammon declined his offer and rang the station to send DS Bass to pick it up from the

Micklock Mercury offices. That will straighten you up Gammon thought as he said goodbye to Andrew Sim and headed back to Bixton.

That evening Gammon had to meet Steve Lineman, Bob and Kev who were ushers at the wedding. They had the final fitting of the top hat and tails before the big day.

They met at Dickens and Greenwood men's outfitters in Bixton. Steve wasn't himself and almost tore Bob's head off when he asked if he was he moody because he was having second thoughts. John was more concerned that he had slept with India, and how would his best mate take that if it came out?

With the suits ready for a week on Saturday, the day of the wedding, they all decided to head back to the Spinning Jenny. All that was except Steve who said he had too much to do. John knew what was bugging Steve, but there was nothing he could do about it, except perhaps to avoid India, at least until the wedding was done and dusted he thought.

Over a week passed and John was feeling better that the Micklock Mercury letter was a fake as he drove into work. His journey was broken when Magic called to say there had been a body found in Clough Dale by an early morning jogger. Magic said he had sent DI Milton and DI Kiernan to investigate and DS Bass was on her way with the forensic team. Gammon told Magic he would go straight there and arrived just as Wally had finished putting the tent up round the grisly scene.

Gammon went straight to DS Bass.

"Sir, this is the gentleman who found the body, Mr Peter Gregory."

"Ok Mr Gregory, I realise this will have been very traumatic for you. Are you ok to answer a few questions?"

Gregory nodded.

"What time did you find the body?"

"It would have been around 7.50am. I usually pass through this part of the wood at that time."

"Where are you running to?"

"Back home to Brichover. I set off at 6.00am from my home in Brichover run to Swinster then down to Clough Dale through the woods then climb back up to Brichover. It's about 7.5 miles in total. I'm a bank manager in Micklock and do a lot of sitting, so the running helps with the fitness you see."

"Did you touch the body, Sir?"

PAY FOR YOUR SIN

"Yes, I am trained in First Aid and thought I might help him, but he was gone I'm afraid."

"Ok Mr Gregory, did you see anybody at all after you left your house this morning?"

"As I came down through Clough Dale before going into the woods I did see a man. He was about six feet one with a swarthy complexion. I said hello, but he looked away."

"Have you ever seen that man before?"

"No, never normally see anyone, Mr Gammon."

"Ok Mr Gregory, my DS will take your details, we may need to speak again."

"Ok, Mr Gammon."

Gammon wandered over to Wally.

"Before you say it John, no I have no information yet. It's too early, well other than carved in the right foot is the letters 'RPF', same as the others."

"Will you be able to tell if the bodies before and this one were done by the same person?"

"Yes, should do, John. I can have it ready for 9.00am tomorrow."

Gammon left the scene telling Milton to arrange a meeting in the incident room for 9.00am the next day.

All Gammon could hope for was that this was a copycat and Tommy Spire was still the killer, if not the brown stuff would really hit the fan.

PAY FOR YOUR SIN

CHAPTER THREE

The following morning Gammon hadn't had much sleep. He knew this could be serious if they had indeed convicted the wrong man.

It was with trepidation that he entered the incident room and walked to the front.

"Ok everyone, some time back I was called to a meeting with Chief Constable Andrew Sim and the editor of the Micklock Mercury. The reason for the meeting was a letter outlining the murders of Amy Lord and Annie Board. The author outlined why they were murdered and that he and not the man we sent to prison was actually the killer."

"I believed this to be a hoax letter from a person wanting his twisted glory for the killings, knowing we have a man serving time for them. That was until yesterday."

"Wally, can you step forward and let us know what you have found please."

"The body was Caucasian about six feet in height. I would say he was late forties or early fifties, with greying blonde hair. The man had been tortured before he died. On the base of his right foot the killer had scrapped 'RPF'. By the way the cuts were put into the man's foot I can almost say categorically that the three murders were all done by the same person. Well at least the artwork."

Gammon's heart sank.

"Do we have a name, Wally?"

"Yes, his dental records tell us his name was Freeman Gillespie and he was the store manager at Fruit and Veg World in Ackbourne."

"Were there any other notes or clues?

PAY FOR YOUR SIN

"Stuffed in his pocket was a blood-soaked piece of paper which said 'SINNER'."

"Any DNA, Wally?"

"No, this was written in the Mr Gillespie's blood."

"Ok, listen up everyone, we may have a miscarriage of justice and I am sure you all realise the consequences of that. I have to inform Chief Constable Sim now, so let's call it a day and get your thinking caps on. DS Bass and DS Yap, you go and see Mr Gillespie's family and break the bad news please."

Gammon knew this could be catastrophic for his career. This wasn't the first time Bixton had been involved in a miscarriage of justice. There was only one way Gammon knew of facing his demons, head on and see what happens. Gammon decided to go and see Andrew Sim to tell him what forensics had found. Gammon arrived at Police Headquarters to see Sim. Sim made him wait almost thirty five minutes before finally seeing him. Sim's PA showed him into Sim's office. A stern faced Andrew Sim sat bolt upright and Gammon could feel this was going to be bad.

"Sit down Gammon."

Gammon sat in the plush leather seat.

"What news have you for me?"

"Not good Sir. John Walvin our forensic manager is quite convinced that the latest body found yesterday matched the same markings on the other two victims, so he is saying they were all done by the same person."

"Well that's our fish well and truly fried Gammon. How the bloody hell could you have got this so wrong?"

PAY FOR YOUR SIN

"With the greatest of respect Sir, you have shadowed this all the way with me and you didn't see past Tommy Spire as the killer."

Sim's face was enraged by Gammon's comments.

"Well Gammon, this is a bloody mess and we will both be lucky to keep our rank."

Sim was raging on about incompetence and how he thought he could trust John, when in life sometimes you get a break. The desk sergeant knocked on Sim's door.

"What is it, Sergeant Phillips?"

"I thought I best let you know they found Tommy Spire dead in Leicester prison this morning. He had hung himself."

The relieve on Sim's face was a picture.

"Thank you, Sergeant."

Sim looked at Gammon.

"Right, this latest case is treated as a new case. The other two murders stay with the deceased Tommy Spire, am I clear Gammon?"

"If you say so, Sir."

"Can't you see man, that's just saved our bacon."

"Just so I have it clear, if we find the guy that really killed three people we are only going to charge him with the latest murder, is that right?"

"Not bloody slow, are you Gammon?"

"Right, I best get ready for a press conference and you get off and get the bloody killer before he does anymore."

"Ok, Sir."

Gammon got back in his car and immediately rang DI Smarty and told him what had happened to Spire and to inform the team that they were only looking for

PAY FOR YOUR SIN

Freeman Gillespie killer, the other two died with Spire.

It was late afternoon when Gammon got back to the station and of course he got twenty questions from Smarty, but that was fine. He wasn't happy with the lie but his boss said that was it, so that was it.

It was almost 5.00pm when Gammon's office phone rang and a strange voice started talking.

"You are DCI Gammon?"

"Yes, who is this?"

"The people who are dead are sinners."

"What had the last man done wrong?"

"He didn't rest on a Sunday and he made people work, that is wrong Mr Gammon."

Gammon detected a slight lisp when the man spoke which might help in solving the case.

"We will get you for these murders, so why don't you give yourself up? You need treatment."

The man laughed and told Gammon to wait for the next one then hung up.

Gammon called Smarty up to his office and told him about the call.

"It appears he is killing to order John, and to the Ten Commandments."

"How the hell do we catch him and maybe there is more than one person doing these things, Dave?"

"I'm calling it a night, you fancy a pint Dave?"

"Sorry mate, not tonight, got to pick the wife up from her sister's, she doesn't like driving in dark nights. When is Steve's wedding?"

"A week on Saturday mate."

"I am guessing you are the best man then?"

PAY FOR YOUR SIN

"Yes, got that job for my sins."

"Right, good night John, see you in the morning."

"Yeah, goodnight Dave."

John left Bixton and headed for the Spinning Jenny. He hadn't heard from Saron in a while now and wasn't sure how to play the situation. It would be a tricky time for her because of last year, and the wedding failure and everything.

John's journey to the Spinning Jenny was to say the least a bit hairy. The roads were quite bad with one or two accidents because of the frozen roads and the light dusting of snow.

He arrived in the pub to see Kev behind the bar, finishing cleaning the pipes and uttering that it was always left to him.

John stood at the bar patiently waiting when he spotted India in the back snug area reading a book with a cup of coffee.

Now what did he do? Make his excuse as Kev hadn't served him yet, or go over and say hello.

John decided on the latter option.

"Hey India, how are you liking this Derbyshire weather?"

"Yes, I walked over hence the furry boots and woolly hat," and she laughed revealing a perfect set of white teeth. She seemed quite relaxed and not in the least bit on edge. Whereas John felt a bit nervous which he put it down to the situation.

"So how are you, Mr Gammon?"

"I'm good thank you."

"Well I did some more on the family tree and I have seen a picture of Jo from an archived photo in the Micklock Mercury. You are correct, it's like looking in the mirror. I will wait until after Christmas then see if I can speak with her sister. Did you say her name is Tracey Rodgers and maybe your friend?"

"Yes, that's correct India and let Steve get the wedding out of the way."

"So, have you had a nice day?"

Kev put John's pint of pedigree on the table and apologised for the wait.

"Yes, it started bad but ended up somewhat better, India. What about you?"

"Yes, good thank you. I got a load more done on the book, so I'm pleased with that. Could I be cheeky and ask for a lift home when you go, John?"

This wasn't what John wanted but felt he had to say yes with the weather so bad.

"I'm just going to have a chat with Kev then will drop you off."

"No rush John, I am quite happy here with my glass of red, my book and that big log fire."

"I'll send you a red wine over, what is it?"

"Merlot, thank you John."

John spent a couple of hours chewing the fat with Kev then told India he was ready. There was nobody in, thank goodness, because of the weather. As he left the car park Imogen Elliot was driving in. Shit, I don't need this he thought. They arrived at India's cottage and she asked him in for a night cap. John declined. He almost weakened but his friendship with Steve was at stake here. He watched India up the drive and safely into her house then set off home pleased with himself and his self-control.

John poured himself a large Jameson's, quickly showered and was in bed with his book and his whisky by 10.45pm. Although was enjoying his book his mind kept wandering to the case, and the fact

PAY FOR YOUR SIN

Tommy Spire, it appeared, had been wrongly committed. Whilst Sim felt that they had both had a get out of jail card it didn't sit right with John.

The following day John drove the scenic route into work. His head was pretty much mush due to the Tommy Spire thing, and India coming into his life. But he knew if he attempted any kind of relationship with her it would ultimately affect Steve his best mate and he was frightened of that. As John rode along he recorded his speech for Steve's wedding, intending to write it down when he got a minute.

Gammon arrived at Bixton at 9.10am. Magic informed him that Chief Constable Sim was in his office with a woman. Crap Gammon thought, the one day I'm a bit late.

Gammon entered his office where Sim and the woman were sat waiting.

111

"Good morning, Sir."

"Yes, good afternoon Gammon, this is Jenny Rose, sorry DCI Jenny Rose. She is coming to work at Bixton alongside you. What I would like you to do is get one of your officers to take Jenny round while we have a little chat."

Gammon was totally confused.

DI Milton was sent to take DCI Rose round the station. As they left, Sim shut the office door.

"What the hell is going on, Sir?"

"Look Gammon, I have to say I felt very let down over the Spire case. I have looked through your records and it appears you have been hasty in your arrests before, so my trust was misplaced."

"Sir, I think that is somewhat harsh, as I ran everything through you first."

"Look Gammon, I don't believe in micro managing. I never have so that is one of the reasons DCI Rose will be working alongside you running the ship."

Gammon tried to butt in, but it was a waste of time Sim was in full verbal bull shit mode.

"DCI Rose will be back in a minute. You probably guessed by the accent she isn't from Derbyshire, she is from the Mid-West. She was married to DS Jude, but they divorced. She has been a police officer for twelve years."

Gammon realised who Jennifer Rose was. She had cracked a high profile case in Sussex. Two brothers had been raping women and stealing their belongings before murdering them. She actual set a honey trap and sorted both the blokes out. Now Gammon knew who she was he felt better about the situation, but he wasn't telling Sim that.

They had just finished when DCI Jennifer Rose walked back in the room. She seemed very assured with herself and oozed confidence, but in a professional manner.

"So what time do you start John?"

"Oh, usually around 8.10am."

"Nearer 9.00am, if this morning is anything to go by Gammon."

Gammon could have punched his lights out, but at least Sim would be bothering DCI Rose, and not him anymore, so it was a win-win situation.

"Ok DCI Gammon, I will take DCI Rose back to get her things sorted and she will see you tomorrow."

"Ok Sir, goodbye. Goodbye Jennifer."

"Call me Jenny, John, it's less formal. I'm looking forward to meeting everyone."

They left Gammon's office and he stood looking over at Losehill covered in snow.

PAY FOR YOUR SIN

He was reflecting on officers that had come and gone for whatever reason and who he had now. DI Lee, DI Smarty, DI Milton, DS Yap, DS Bass DS Winnipeg and PC Magic on the front desk. He maybe did need some help so maybe Sim was right. Gammon just didn't like the way Sim had gone about it.

Gammon called down to the front desk and told Magic to make sure all the station were in the incident room at 9.00am for an announcement.

John decided to call Saron on the way home to see if she had calmed down with wedding being on Saturday. He would have liked her to go with him. She was still frosty with him and said she could get cover to go and see Steve get married. But she had to get back because Pippa's Frozen Foods were having their Christmas Party that day at the Tow'd Man. John was disappointed but understood. He said he would see her in the church where they were being married at 11.40am at St James Church in Puddle Dale.

He decided to go straight home he didn't want a load of beer before he settled Jenny Rose in at work.

Roger Glazeback had just finished milking with his lad as John pulled in front of his cottage.

"Hi John, you ok? We don't normally see you at this time of night."

"Steve Lineman is getting married on Saturday, so I need to get my speech done."

"I was saying to the wife that it was a bit quick after losing Jo and the baby in that dreadful fire."

"Know what you mean Roger, but he seems happy and I am sure Jo would have wanted that for him mate."

PAY FOR YOUR SIN

"Guess so John, right good night mate."

"Yes, goodnight Roger."

Roger's son wasn't the talkative type and had already set off for home while John and Roger were talking.

Once inside John poured himself a large Jameson's and made himself a bowl of soup. It was that time of the year when like everybody who had lost family start thinking about previous Christmas's spent with their loved ones. Although John hadn't spent that much time with his family over the years because of his time in London, and his marriage to Lindsay, it didn't mean his thoughts weren't with them.

Now, what did he have a year ago? He had a beautiful fiancée and a future mapped out, but his stupidity meant he lost Saron and almost lost his life. All John could hope for was a better Christmas this year.

He sat down to write his best man speech, but felt like he was a hypocrite having slept with what will ultimately turn out to be Jo Wickets identical twin sister. He wrote the usual things about Steve, but by bed time he still hadn't finished his speech, and was surrounded by screwed up pieces of paper that resembled a marshmallow moat round his feet.

His best bet was bed and worry about the speech the next night.

The following morning he arrived early with the full intention of announcing DCI Rose to the team. His office desk once again resembled a war zone with all the paperwork. He started to work his way through it. DI Smarty knocked on his door.

"It's almost 9.00am, John."

PAY FOR YOUR SIN

"On my way, Dave."

Everybody was in the incident room. DCI Rose entered. She was slim with auburn hair and wore a fitted suit with a skirt cut just above her knees. She had a magnetic smile with a perfect set of polished teeth.

"Ok everybody, as you are aware we have been somewhat light on the ground, so first of all I wish to introduce you to a new addition to our team here at Bixton. DCI Jennifer Rose. I will just go round the room and ask you to announce yourself for DCI Rose."

"You first, Carl."

"DI Carl Milton."

"DI Dave Smarty."

"DI Peter Lee."

"DI Daniel Kiernan, ma'am."

"DS John Winnipeg."

"DS Kate Bass."

"PC Magic, ma'am, front desk."

"Very pleased to meet you all."

"Over there is head of Forensics, John Walvin."

"And you too, John. Just to give you a bit of my history. I was born and raised in the States Mid-West. I married an English Police officer. That didn't work out, so I joined the police in London and worked my way up the greasy poll. Then this opportunity came along. I met DCI Gammon and I am very pleased to be sharing responsibilities for the cases here at Bixton. I am sure John won't mind me saying, but I am guessing I will get the paperwork side, as I can see John is not a fan of paperwork."

This made the team laugh and Gammon gave Rose a wry smile.

"Ok nice things over with, welcome to the team DCI Rose. The situation at the moment is we have a murderer loose in the Peak District. This is what he does," and Gammon showed her the pictures of the feet of the victims with 'RPF' carved in their feet.

"I am going to be open and honest with the team, but not a word of this is breathed outside this room."

"I believe Tommy Spire was arrested and subsequently charged and convicted for the murders of Amy Lord and Annie Board. The real killer has now killed again. This victim was Freeman Gillespie a manager at a popular fruit and veg shop. The killer states he was killed for working on the Sabbath and making other people do the same. Annie Board was killed because as a young girl she stole from her employer. Amy Lord was murdered for having an affair. So, you can see the pattern emerging. We have to get this man before much more damage can be heaped on our community."

"DS Bass and DI Kiernan, I want you to concentrate on Freeman Gillespie's bank accounts; anything unusual etc."

"DI Lee and DI Milton, pay a visit to the man's workplace see who his friends are, see if he socialised etc."

"Winnipeg and DI Smarty, look into the person who found Freeman, do some door knocking see what you can shake out of the tree."

"Ok everybody, it's the weekend tomorrow, with Christmas Eve on Sunday. I hope you and your families have a great Christmas and thanks for your efforts all year. Sadly, I do need everyone back on the 28th as we have a murder to solve, so not a long break for you all."

Gammon left the meeting and showed DCI Rose to what was DCI Dirk's office.

PAY FOR YOUR SIN

"That's grand John. Listen before we start today, I just wanted to say I am here to help, there is no hidden agenda. I was told your work load; the death of DI Scooper and your very bad car accident last Christmas time had taken a lot out of you. What I don't want is us to get off on the wrong foot. If for any reason I am standing on your toes you let me know."

"Same for me, Jenny."

"Great, right let's get this killer caught."

The first day was always a bit of a challenge for any DCI so Gammon left Jenny Rose to it, knowing he had a shed load of paperwork, and a speech to write for Steve's wedding the next day. He played back what he had recorded in the car, but it all sounded false so he decided to do it from the heart.

It was about 5.35pm when DCI Rose came through to say goodnight.

"You will like Cambridge Lodge, Jenny, nice people and a proper pukka place to stay with fantastic views."

"Sounds great, John. Listen, good luck with your wedding tomorrow and have a lovely Christmas."

"What are you doing Jenny, for Christmas lunch?"

"Unsure really, I was going to look on internet tonight to see if I could get a meal."

"Here let me phone Doreen at the Spinning Jenny. I am sure she will do you a Christmas dinner."

John called Doreen and explained the situation.

"Of course love, if she doesn't mind having it with me and Kev about 2.00pm. I've got fifty five in at 12.15pm."

"Is that ok, Jenny?"

"Yes, that's great. Tell her thank you."

PAY FOR YOUR SIN

"Right have a lovely time, John."

Gammon felt a bit bad not asking her for a drink, but he was going to see Saron and the last thing he needed was more complications. He was also hoping she might ask him over for Christmas dinner at the Tow'd Man, so he hadn't arranged anything.

John arrived at the Tow'd Man and Saron was prepping in the kitchen with Donna Fringe working the bar. Saron spoke but she wasn't gushing towards John.

"Just thought I would pop in to see if you might come to Steve's night do."

"I told you John, I will be there at the wedding, then I have to get back. I'm sure you will have enough followers to enjoy the day and night John, and she turned round to carry on prepping.

Get on with it he thought so popped his head in the bar ordered a pint and sat talking to Donna.

"How is Saron, Donna?"

"She is ok, John. Why?"

"Oh, we aren't getting on great. I was hoping she would ask me over for Christmas dinner."

"We are going to her Mum's. She has invited me, Tracey Rodgers and Carol Lestar and her Mum. But I'm not sure if Carol is going she hasn't been too well this last week."

"Looks like beans on toast for me then."

"Yeah, like John Gammon with all his suitors having beans on toast, who are you kidding?"

"Don't believe the hype, Donna."

John had another couple of pints and went home to finish his speech. On the way he called Steve to say he would pick

PAY FOR YOUR SIN

him up at 11.00am and they could have a quick drink in the Limping Duck before heading to St James Church for the ceremony. Steve seemed a bit off with John. John put it down to nerves so rang off and carried on with his speech. He was finding it tough and he knew why. What was worrying John was, did Steve know why?

The following morning John showered made himself a bacon sandwich and checked his e-mails hoping Fleur may have contacted him, but there was nothing.

His cleaner Phyllis Swan had ironed his shirt and polished his shoes. She really was a gem John thought. John arrived at Tracey Rodgers where Steve had stopped the night and popped outside. Steve came out. John thought Steve always carried a suit well, he had a good physique.

"Morning mate."

"Yeah morning John."

"Cheer up mate, it's your wedding day."

"I'll be honest mate, I wish you hadn't told me about that girl who looks like Jo. I asked around Hartington and the vicar, Matthew Spouncer, said he was taken aback when he saw her. He said he shouldn't believe in ghosts but she was the nearest thing."

"Look mate, if I hadn't of told you and you either bumped into her or somebody else told you, what would you have thought of me?"

"No, I know mate. Have you seen her since that night in the pub?"

Now John either lied to Steve or this would all come crashing down. He decided a white lie might be the best option.

PAY FOR YOUR SIN

"No mate, I haven't. Look forget her. She isn't Jo, and you are about to get married."

"You are right John, let's have a few whiskies."

"What are you doing about a honeymoon?"

"I have treated us two four weeks sailing the Western Caribbean."

"What about the pub mate?"

"Tracey and Carol Lestar are running it, and Tracey is going to stay there so there is somebody on the premises."

Steve was throwing his money around like a man with no hands, and Imogen was loving it John thought.

They had two double brandies in the Limping Duck. Steve was getting the usual stick from the blokes in there about not turning up. By now he had lightened up but John still had that nagging doubt.

They arrived at St James Church in Puddle Dale and John checked he had the ring before they walked down the aisle to the front pew.

John caught a glimpse of Saron and smiled. She didn't reciprocate but she was thinking about this time last year John thought.

The bride was customarily late by fifteen minutes. Then the organist struck up the wedding march and Imogen came in. She was given away by an old friend of her father's. The church was quite full and had been decorated by Cheryl and Jackie. The flowers were stunning, all white and pink everywhere you looked.

The vicar stood at the front.

"Dearly beloved, we are gathered here today etc"

The vicar then reminded Steve and Imogen of the importance of their vows.

PAY FOR YOUR SIN

He then said the vows and the giving of the rings. He then pronounced them man and wife.

"You may kiss the bride."

Deep down John knew Steve wasn't happy, but there was nothing he could do. There was the usual throwing of confetti. John stood with the head bridesmaid, a girl in her mid-thirties called Amelia Oakley, apparently a big friend of Imogen when she was working away. She was a nice girl not a stunning beauty, but nice figure and pleasant.

Once back at the Star Inn the room had been decked out professionally. Steve said that was how Imogen wanted it. John thought I bet Steve is paying for it though.

It finally came round to John's speech.

John clinked his knife handle against his glass to get everyone's attention.

"Ok you lot, here we go, my bit. Is it warm in here or, is it me?" he said loosening his tie.

"Ladies and gentleman, and of course any scallies that Steve invited. Present company accepted Bob."

That got the first laugh.

"I would like to thank the head bridesmaid Amelia, and the other two bridesmaids, Julie and Saffron, and of course little Willie the page boy who I am sure you all thought was brilliant."

John raised his glass and they all followed.

"They say a problem shared is a problem solved, but I would imagine Steve is thinking that it may have doubled the problem having me speak about him."

"I was quite nervous when Steve asked me to be his best man, knowing that the task required a bit of creativity, a little patience and some ingenuity. I thought well, that's me well and truly stuffed!"

"Before we get to the stories I should really point out what a fantastic, good looking and funny person my mate Steve is, but I don't feel comfortable telling blatant lies in front of the vicar, so I think we should move on."

"We have been best friends since starting junior school together, a good few years ago I might add."

"Steve's drinking, having been in the navy, is legendary. So, for him to be taking a pub and becoming a landlord seemed the obvious route for him."

"You can talk, Porky," Steve shouted.

"No heckling please Mr Lineman, or this little speech could get worse."

"I spoke with Imogen's aunty in church today, and she said it only seems five minutes ago since Imogen was going to bed with her dummy. Funny how history repeats itself, Imogen," he said looking over at Steve's bride.

"Well I have probably bored you all now, so I will just say Steve, you have a beautiful, kind, considerate, generous and loving bride and Imogen you have …… well, Steve."

The whole room laughed as John sat down.

"Whoops, almost forgot," he said standing back up.

"Please join in me in raising your glasses to a happy and contented life together. The bride and groom, Mr and Mrs Lineman."

With all the speeches done. John sneaked outside to call Saron. The phone rang five times before she eventually picked it up.

"Hi, I wondered if you wanted to come back tonight for the night do?"

PAY FOR YOUR SIN

"No, I'm fine thank you. I need to go. I am busy," and the she hung up.

He was feeling a bit down. It appeared Saron had decided they weren't to be an item anymore. John wandered back in and Steve and Imogen were having the first dance to 'Simply the Best' by Tina Turner, for some reason Steve always liked this song. John sat at one of the tables on the perimeter of the dance floor. Tracey Rodgers came over and sat with John.

"You ok, John?"

"Yes fine, Tracey."

"You could have fooled me. You and Steve don't seem right, what's a matter?"

Now did John tell her about her potential sister or not?

"Look, I need to tell you something that may shock you."

"Go on then, Mr Secretive."

"I think you have a sister you don't know about, Tracey."

"What?"

"Don't be daft."

"No listen, there is a girl living in Hartington who is the exact double of Jo, and I mean exact double. She is an author who came to the Peak District to write a book which she penned as 'My Lost Sister'. I have spoken with her and got to know her. Tracey, she is Jo's double. She said she was adopted that she believed she had relations in the area. She actually had been to Jo and Steve's house, obviously burnt down."

"John, are you sure it's not a scam?"

"Well I have spent many years in the detective game, and I know a chancer when I see one."

"Have you told Steve?"

"I had to."

PAY FOR YOUR SIN

"So that's why he is all upset?"

"Don't say anything, but I walked in on him crying last night. He wouldn't tell me what the matter was. I just assumed the occasion was getting to him."

"John, take me to meet this girl."

"Ok, be at my house for 10.00am tomorrow."

"What does she know?"

"Everything, but she assured me she didn't want to upset Steve's wedding day, so would keep a low profile until after the wedding."

"Ok, I will be at yours at 10.00am, unless I get asked for a sleep over tonight with you."

She laughed and left John pondering.

John knew he had to shake himself out of his current feeling of woe, so he asked Shelley Etchings for a dance.

"Take her lad, saves my legs."

"Thanks, Jack."

"You ok, John? You don't seem yourself."

"Yeah fine, just a lot on with work, Shelley."

"I thought you might have had some beauty on your arm."

"Who, Saron?"

"Sorry John, but I think that ship sailed mate. Now Sheba is hooked up with Phil Sterndale the beauties are getting thin on the ground, hey lad."

"Give over, Shelley."

"Yeah, you are right, bloody John Gammon always comes up smelling of roses," and she laughed.

The wedding seemed to be a success. John ended up with the last dance with Tracey Rodgers who was determined to get her comment of a sleep over in place. By now John wasn't bothered he had hardly spoken to Steve, and Imogen hadn't spoken to him at all. The taxis started arriving and Tracey said she would share with John, which caused Bob to nod to Jack in a nod, nod, wink, wink sort of comment.

There was only one way this was going and within minutes John and Tracey were stripped and making love. First on the kitchen table, then the sofa, then in front of the log burner.

They eventually went to bed at almost 3.00am the following morning. John woke at 8.15am Tracey was sitting up reading John's book.

"About time, I thought you were never going to wake up. John, I am kind of excited by this, having lost my only sister and to find I might have a sister I didn't know about.

John knew what she meant, but just hoped it never got out that he had slept with India. He had done some stupid things he thought but this one took the biscuit.

"Come on, I will take you to the Victoriana Café in Biffin by Hittington."

"Oh, I have heard about that, they say it's fabulous, John."

"Yeah, Lisa Tink told me about it."

"I like Lisa, she is such a kind-hearted soul."

"Yeah, Lisa and Jim have a lovely place called Cambridge Lodge. One or two from work have stopped there."

They arrived in Biffin and the Victoriana Café. All the staff were dressed as milking parlour maids and it was all decorated with everything to do with old farming methods.

PAY FOR YOUR SIN

A pleasant you girl asked John and Tracey what they would like.

"I'll take the full English please, with a strong black coffee."

"For you Madam?"

"Could I have the Eggs Benedict and a green tea please?"

"Coming right up."

They sat talking and Tracey said she was surprised that John had been with Anouska on his wedding eve. John was surprised that she knew, but small villagers don't keep secrets he thought.

Straight after breakfast John paid and they headed to India's place hoping she was in. They walked up the drive and Tracey clung onto John's arm.

"I am excited but also apprehensive, John."

"That's understandable, Tracey. Just don't be shocked if she opens the door."

John knocked twice and India came to the door. Tracey took one look and fainted in John's arms.

"Who is this John? Is she ok?"

"This is Tracey Rodgers, Jo's sister and quite possibly yours India."

"Bring her inside, let me get her a glass of water."

Tracey slowly came round and looked at India in amazement.

"I don't believe this."

"I know, John told me. I have never seen a picture of Jo. Have you got one?"

"Actually I have, it was a day trip somewhere."

Tracey rummaged in her handbag and pulled out a picture of her and Jo.

The silence was deafening as India took in that this person was almost certainly her identical twin sister. India was overcome with emotion and just started crying

PAY FOR YOUR SIN

Tracey comforted her and she started crying.

After a few minutes John said he had an idea.

"I shouldn't do this normally, but what if I take a sample of both your hair and see if we have a DNA family match? I could do this at work if you want."

Both girls said yes please.

Both girls got samples and put them in separate freezer bags for John to take. He had just put them in his inside pocket when his phone rang.

"John Gammon."

"Hello Sir, sorry to bother you but looks like we have another victim."

"Where Magic?"

"Sparrow Dale Sir, a school party doing the Duke of Edinburgh award found the body on the stepping stones crossing the river. I have informed John Walvin and his team. They are on the way. DI Milton was in anyway so he rang DI Lee and they have gone to the scene."

"Ok Magic, good work."

"I'm sorry ladies, but I am going to have to go to work, something came up."

"Do you want to stop a bit Tracey and I will run you back to your place?"

"That would be lovely, India."

"Thanks John," they shouted as he left for Sparrow Dale.

Sparrow Dale was a tourist hot spot set in a deep valley with the river and a weir running through it with small stepping stones that people used to get from one side of the valley to the other. Gammon rang back to Magic to arrange for some beat lads to cordon off the passage to the stepping stones with so many tourists about.

PAY FOR YOUR SIN

Gammon arrived at the scene and spoke with DI Lee.

"We have taken statements, Sir. A young kid found the body, but the teacher was soon on the scene and gave us a full statement."

"Ok, well done Peter. Who is Milton talking to?"

"I think it's the Peak Park Ranger." Gammon wandered over and introduced himself. Gammon showed his warrant card.

"This is Myra Coolby, she is the local Park Ranger, Sir."

"Pleased to meet you, Myra."

"I was just saying to your officer, we have a lot of people not allowed to enter the area, and some have come a long way. How long will you be?"

Gammon didn't like her tone.

"We will be as long as it takes to collate all the evidence to this poor man's death. Now if you don't mind, please step the other side of the police tape."

Gammon carried on across the stepping stones to the other side of the weir to where Wally had set his tent up.

John put his head inside.

"Get out John," shouted Wally but then again he always did so John knew what he was doing.

"Before you ask John, nothing yet other than 'RPF' carved on his right foot like the rest. Yes, I will have something more for your when I am back at work."

"Which is when, Wally?"

"Same as you, day after Boxing Day, the 27th. I will have had enough of wrapping paper and turkey by then, John."

Gammon smiled and thanked Wally.

PAY FOR YOUR SIN

"Ok Carl, you and Peter get off. Just tell the Sergeant holding the crowds back that once Wally says it's ok they can resume as normal, but not before.

"Ok Sir, see you the day after Boxing Day."

Gammon also left and decided to go home and finish his book 'Grove'. He had read the first two in the trilogy; 'Looking For Shona' and 'The Hurt Of Yochana' so he was now quite engrossed in the final book, 'Grove'.

John arrived home but quickly called DCI Rose to let her know about the events. He poured a large Jameson's and cut a piece of Christmas Cake that Phyllis Swan had made for him, placing a piece of Lancashire cheese on top. This was something his Mum always did when he was small. He thought it odd but now he loved it.

John settled down in front of a blazing
log burner. Looking toward the garden he
could see it was starting to snow quite
heavily. So much so that the view just
looked like a white blanket to stare at.

It was 12.10am when he finally finished
the book with some surprise he hadn't
expected from the Egan family. John
called it a night and fell into bed and was
soon asleep.

Christmas Day and John was at a loose
end. He got up trying to decide what to do.
They had about four inches of snow, but
Roger Glazeback had dug out for the milk
tanker all the way to the road.

John decided to make himself a bacon
sandwich and sat feeling somewhat sorry
for himself. He had hoped a year would
heal the pain Saron felt, and they would

have by now had their relationship back on track, but it hadn't worked out like that.

He cut two slice of thick bread and grilled to sizeable pieces of Phil Sterndale's bacon he had given him from one of his pigs.

Whilst the bacon sandwich and the coffee were comforting it didn't alter the fact that his life was a mess.

He had slept with his best friend's dead wife's sister. Thinking about it he thought that was actually both sisters Tracey and India. Saron was very cold towards him and seemed to want her own life. Anouska hadn't been in touch although he never missed sending money for little Anka. His sister Fleur never kept in touch. His Chief Constable Andrew Sim had lost faith in him, hence the reason he now had DCI Rose alongside him. Life was just crap at the minute, then to top it all his mate was leaving the Spinning Jenny to retire. What else could possibly go wrong John thought?

John decided to put his walking boots and got to Hittington church for the morning service. He hadn't done that since his Mum used to take him and Adam on Christmas Day every year.

John slipped into a pew at the back. The church was quite full as the vicar made his way up to the pulpit.

"Christmas is a time to remember loved ones. To be kind and thoughtful to others, to put people first before yourselves. Would you all stand for 'Once in Royal David's City'."

John stood, and he had no sooner got the first line of the carol out of his mouth when he felt a dig in his ribs. It was India looking like some kind of super model with her dark hair hanging from beneath a coney fur hat. She had a fur coat on with big fur boots and that smile that absolutely melted John.

She whispered, "Are you on your own?"

"Yes," John said.

India came from the pew behind and stood with John sharing the carol song sheet.

John wasn't sure he wanted that because one or two of the parishioners remembered Jo, and there was John Steve Lineman's best mate standing with somebody who was almost identical. The vicar did the service and they sang the final carol 'Away in a Manger'. Then the vicar sent the choir boys round with a collection plate.

John stepped outside with India.

"So where are you having Christmas dinner, John?"

John felt embarrassed to say he had nowhere to go, so tried to off-set it by saying he had a mountain of paperwork to do so would just grab a sandwich.

"I won't let you do that Christmas Day. Dinner is on and you are coming to mine. No arguing, that's the least I can do for all you have done for me."

John felt quite warm inside as they strolled up to India's rented cottage. The snow was just above their ankles. Christmas is such a romantic time John thought.

Once inside the cottage, the smell of the fire and the Christmas tree all brightly lit with coloured lights, put John at the point of what the hell I am doing nothing wrong.

"Sit down John and I will pour you a drink while I finish off the dinner."

"Are you sure I can't help you, India?"

PAY FOR YOUR SIN

"No, I'm fine. I enjoy cooking and don't get the chance to cook for anyone, so this is kind of a treat for me."

India came back with a large glass of red wine and John sat on the settee.

"Here John, have a look at my latest book and tell me what you think. Dinner will only be twenty minutes."

John sat reading India's book and became quite engrossed to the point of not wanting to put it down. Twenty minutes flew by.

"Dinner is out, John."

He carefully closed the draft copy of India's book and headed to the dining room. Another lovely room with an old style cast iron range. India, who was clearly very arty had decorated it in just red and silver with a small Christmas tree in the window.

"John, this is so nice. I haven't had a Christmas with anyone since Brodie and I split."

"Were you married?"

"No, engaged and we sort of lived together. He worked away a lot as he was a geologist for a big oil company and travelled everywhere That's how I took up writing. For the first two and a half years I travelled with him. One minute Scotland, then Norway, then Peru and all over South America. I spent a lot of time in hotel rooms while he worked, so writing kind of fitted well into my life."

"Have you been successful?"

"Yes luckily, did you ever see The Darkest Shadow? It was on television about two years ago, then they made a film but they called the film 'The Needy'."

PAY FOR YOUR SIN

"Never saw the TV program, but saw the film, it was incredible. Didn't Will Smith play the lead?"

"That's the one."

"Wow, well done you."

"Thank you."

"What happened to you and Brody?"

"Long story, but let's say it wasn't to be."

John sensed she didn't want to talk anymore on the subject.

"Wow, this is a lovely dinner India, thank you."

"It's my pleasure, the way you have helped me."

With dinner finished John helped clear the table and India poured two large ports for them. She asked John if he fancied watching Scrunch and Plunket.

"That's the latest Matt Damon film."

"Yeah, would love to."

They settled on the settee and India lay her head on John's shoulder. What a lovely day he thought, possibly one of the nicest Christmas Days he had in many years. The only thing still worrying John was his friendship with Steve. He knew Steve wasn't right about India, but what could he do? Steve was now married, he was single and India was single as far as he knew.

The film finished at 6.10pm and through the little cottage windows John could see it was snowing quite heavy.

"Where is the nearest pub John, that might be open? It would be nice to go and have a walk in the snow and a couple of drinks."

"Well if we walk about ten minutes back up the lane and take the big field we will come to Biffin by Hittington. I think the

PAY FOR YOUR SIN

Black Bess will be open now until about 10.00pm, they usually are."

"Come on then John, let's go."

It suited John. He knew not many would be out Christmas Day night and not many locals were left in Biffin anyway. It had been taken over by outsiders as the locals called them.

They walked over to the Black Bess in almost four inches of snow. India was such good fun John thought as they snowballed and played like children in the fields carpeted in snow.

They finally arrived at the pub. John was surprised that it was quite busy, and an old guy in a flat cap was playing Christmas Carols on an upright piano in the corner.

"John, this is a really special day for me, thank you."

"Hey, it should be me thanking you. I am having a wonderful day."

It was the landlord's birthday and a middle-aged lady was going round the pub with a big card for everyone to sign. She gave it to John and India. It was then that the twenty four hour policeman came into his mind when he noticed the name. 'Happy Birthday Roger Patrick Fryer'. 'RPF' John thought. He signed the card but made a mental note.

"Hey John, good to see you."

"Blimey Steve, hardly recognised you with the new hair-cut and the stubble. This is India Green, a friend," which he emphasised to Steve.

Steve Condray took a double take, but John could see he was too polite to say what he was thinking, which was she looked like Jo Wickets. Steve stuttered as he tried to introduce his girlfriend whilst staring at India.

PAY FOR YOUR SIN

"Pleased to meet you, John. I have heard a lot about you."

John smiled.

"Have you two had a nice Christmas, Steve?"

"It's been great John, what about you?"

He stopped short of saying you two.

"Yes good, thank you."

"Has Steve and Imogen had a honeymoon?"

"Yes, gone on a Caribbean cruise."

"Alright for some, I was working Christmas Day. Dad can't do much now, but he knows how to tell me how to do things," and Steve laughed.

"So, where are you from India and what a lovely name?" Fiona remarked.

"London but I write books, so rented a cottage for a year. I thought the tranquillity might inspire me for my latest book."

"Ooh, what's it called? I will get it when it's published."

"Well at the minute it's called 'My Lost Sister', but I do tend to change titles and my agent may also."

"All sounds interesting, India."

"Thank you, Fiona."

The girls carried on chatting. Steve saw his opportunity to interrogate John about India.

"Blimey John, she is Jo Wickets double. What does your mate think?"

"You have it all wrong. She is just a friend."

"Yeah, pull the other one, it's got bells on John."

John was cursing his luck bumping into somebody who knew Jo Wickets.

The night ended at 10.30pm when the pianist finished and the landlord called last orders. John and India said their goodbyes and headed back across the fields to India's cottage.

As they opened the oak door leading to the living room the warmth of the room hit them. India turned and kissed John. John ungracefully pulled away.

"India, I don't think I should be getting involved."

Feeling hurt India questioned, "Why?"

"Look, I know it sounds stupid, but Steve Lineman is my best mate, and if Jo Wickets is indeed your identical twin sister then it will hurt him for sure."

"But he has remarried, John?"

"I know, but I am sure it was on the rebound. Since I told him about you, he has been in a state of despair, even on his wedding day."

"Ok, the bed in the spare room is made up. I'm going to bed."

John lay in bed in the spare room thinking what a plank he was. Men would have given their right arms to be with India, and he had ostracised her.

The following morning John left a note on the kitchen table before heading home.

'Dear India

Thank you for a wonderful Christmas Day which I eventually ruined, for which I am truly sorry about. It's nothing to do with you. You are a kind, considerate beautiful girl. It's just that I need to get my head round things.

Thanks again

John xx'

PAY FOR YOUR SIN

CHAPTER FOUR

John walked up the lane to his car when his phone rang. It was DCI Rose.

"Hi John, what are you doing?"

"Not a lot, why Jenny?"

"Just I have had an idea on the case and wondered if you fancied helping me for a few hours."

"Where?"

"Oh sorry, here at Bixton, I'm at work."

"Ok, give me an hour and I will be with you."

John got back to the cottage and quickly showered and changed then headed into work.

Di Trimble was on the front desk.

"Blimey, what are you doing here on Boxing Day?"

"I could say the same to you, Sir. DCI Rose said to tell you she is in room one. Would you like a coffee, Sir?"

"Great Di, nice and strong, no milk or sugar please."

John entered the room. Rose had her lap top and numerous files open.

"Oh, hi John, thanks for coming. I decided to look at anybody with the initials 'RPF'. They may be on our data base, just concentrating on Derbyshire and the Peak District."

"What have you got so far?"

"I have Roland Patrick Finney, armed robbery five years ago, came out of Leicester eighteen months ago. Ruby Preston Fullmore, con woman, she was convicted and served three years eleven years ago. This one caught my interest. Remember that game show in the early nineties called 'Do It Wrong and Forfeit'?

PAY FOR YOUR SIN

The host on that was Ricky Peter Flag, well that was the name he was convicted on, his stage name was Bobby King."

"I remember him, he was done for sexual harassment, wasn't he?"

"Yes, he always denied it but got four years at his court case. He swore revenge on the do-gooders of society and people who had done wrong and got away with it. He was released eight years ago and is a vicar in Brichover. He now calls himself the Reverend Andrew Able."

"We may have hit gold with that one. He has motive, the initials on the feet are his, and it appears the killings are some kind of religious thing."

They carried on looking through records and John spotted a company called Retro Parts Ford, Managing Director, Alistair Mackay. He was handed a ten year sentence when one of his employees was made to fit a part on an old Ford Consul which he knew was wrong. A witness at the trial said the employee who was killed had told Mackay that it was dangerous, but he had told him to fit it. He was severely burnt in the ensuing fire but lived in agony for two days before dying.

By 4.00pm they had gone through the data base and decided that the vicar Andrew Able and Alistair Mackay would be worth a look.

"Ok John, let's have a meeting in the morning and get the team involved. Thanks for coming in over the holiday."

"No big problem, Jenny. If it stops any more people getting hurt then it's a win-win."

"Ok John, thanks again, see you in the morning."

Gammon had a quick chat with Di Trimble. He had known Di for many years and rarely saw her as she normally did the night shift on the front desk.

John got in his car and decided to pop and see Doreen and Kevin. He placed his phone on its bracket and plugged it in. He hadn't noticed it had run out of battery and there were four missed calls from India and two from Saron. Now what, he thought? He decided to call Saron first. She seemed quite buoyant.

"What did you do Christmas Day?"

"Not a lot."

"Did you cook?"

"No, just a cheese sandwich."

"What and nothing to drink?"

John hated lying but knew the consequences if he didn't.

"A couple of Jameson's while watching the telly, why?"

"Just wondered, only Fiona Scott who is seeing Steve Condray, said you were with a pretty girl in the Black Bess at Biffin by Hittington, but she must have been mistaken."

"Anyway, best get on, busy night tonight with the Christmas raffle," and Saron hung up.

Shit he thought. For the first time he had done nothing wrong. He had slept alone but he knew Saron knew more than she had said. How did he explain this he thought? What he did know was, he best wide berth Saron for a few weeks to let things calm down.

Next he phoned India.

"Hey, you ignoring me?"

"Sorry, I let my phone battery run down and I've been into work."

"Just wanted to thank you for a lovely day, and to apologise for my immature way last night. I do understand John. I hope we can meet again when things settle down."

"Thanks India, it is awkward but yes I will give you a call when the dust settles."

John felt a bit relieved as he pulled into the Spinning Jenny. He entered the pub and didn't know the two people behind the bar. The man was about six feet one, stocky build, with curly dark hair and was wearing a sparkly waistcoat over his white shirt. The lady was slim, very pretty with an infectious smile.

"Good evening, Sir."

John wasn't used to this in his local.

"Yes, good evening."

"What can I get you?"

"I'll have a pint of Pedigree please."

Just then Kev came into the bar.

"Hey John, meet Lindsay and Wez Beardmore, they will be taking over in two weeks when we retire."

"Oh, pleased to meet you. So, are you that famous detective, John?"

"Not sure about famous Lindsay, but yes I am a detective."

"Wow Wez, we have a famous detective drinking in our pub. Wait until I tell them in Barnsley."

"Do you come a lot?"

"Yes, a bit. It's near to where I live and have known Kev and Doreen for years."

"Come a lot Lindsay, he is flippin' here more than me!"

"Your nose is growing, Kev."

Kev laughed at John's comment.

"Come on lad, come and sit next to the fire with me."

"So that's it then, mate."

"Yeah, but we will still call for a drink."

"Plenty to do in retirement?"

"I have loads to do and the time is right mate."

PAY FOR YOUR SIN

"We are thinking of having our leaving do a week on Saturday. I have booked Tony Maloney's disco; the bar will be cheap and our Doreen is putting food on."

"Blimey mate, it won't be the same."

"It will be good John. We looked at a lot of people and this couple are young and keen. I am sure they will be good for the pub and the community."

John stayed until 9.30pm then decided to make his way back to his cottage.

The following morning he remembered he had the two hair samples. As soon as he arrived at work he spoke with Wally.

"Blimey, now I am doing jobs on the side for the gaffer."

"Ha-ha, very funny Wally, I owe you one."

"I will have the results for you by lunchtime, mate."

"Are we still having the meeting at 9.00am?"

"Yes mate."

"Ok see you there, John."

Gammon went back to his office and had a quick word with DCI Jenny Rose who was engrossed in John's paperwork.

"I see you found my weak spot, Jenny."

"Bloody hell John, how do you get so far behind?"

"Always have, I find it a real pain to be honest."

"Thanks for yesterday. Let's see what comes up in meeting in the incident room at 9.00am, John."

"Ok, see you down there."

All the staff assembled and John led the meeting.

"Ok everyone, let's go through what we have. As you are all aware, my directive is that Tommy Spire, who committed suicide in prison, still carries the can for Amy Lord and Annie Bird. I know what you are all thinking but we have no choice, that directive has come from the top. So that leaves us with Freeman Gillespie and Hayden Tusker. Myself and DCI Rose spent yesterday trawling through convicted criminals living in Derbyshire. We came up with four but two we considered maybe of interest. These people had the initials 'RPF'."

"DI Kiernan and DS Bass, I want you to bring in the Reverend Andrew Able, formerly known as Bobby King, and real name Ricky Peter Flag. He is the vicar at St Marks Church in Brichover. When you get him here give me a shout and we will interview him with you two present."

"DS Winnipeg and DI Milton, you bring in Alistair Mackay, former Managing Director at Retro Parts Ford, now living in sheltered accommodation in Micklock after his release from prison. He lives at 16 Stinton Court Bank Road, Micklock. Again, bring him in and I will interview him with you both. Offer them both a solicitor."

"DI Lee and DI Smarty, take a look at the back ground to these people; usual stuff, bank accounts, any further run-ins with the police. Just look for anything that might be incriminating."

"Sir?"

"Yes, DS Bass."

"Are we not looking into the first two victims at all?"

"Look, I know this goes against the grain, but we have to do what the hierarchy want, DS Bass."

"Ok thanks everybody, let's get going."

"John, don't you feel we are wide open if the press get hold of this?"

PAY FOR YOUR SIN

"Yes, I do but Chief Constable Sim told me that's how he wants it."

"You do know if this gets out he won't be there for you, John?"

"He won't have to be, Jenny. I recorded it on my phone."

"You little tinker, John."

"There is one thing I have learned, Jenny, every gaffer I have had since I came back to the Peak District has given me an umbrella in the sunshine, and taken it away when it rained."

Jenny laughed, "What a great analogy, John."

"Right, let me get back to your paperwork."

"Tell you what, you do half and I'll do half."

"Ok John, sounds good to me."

Gammon took his half to his office and started the torture of paperwork. By

2.00pm he had finished, just as Magic said DS Bass had the Reverend Andrew Able and his solicitor were in interview room one.

"Ok Magic I'm on my way down."

Gammon entered interview room one and DS Bass started the tape running introducing everyone. DI Kiernan sat next to Gammon, opposite Andrew Able and his solicitor Peter Tuft of Tuft and Sligoe, Manchester solicitors, which Gammon thought was a bit odd.

"Mr Able, may I call you Andrew?"

Able nodded to say that was ok.

"The reason for the interview today is your name came up on our data-base. I am assuming you are aware of the horrific murders that have taken place of late in the Peak District?"

Able said he was aware of the dreadful murders through the media.

PAY FOR YOUR SIN

"I wondered could you look at these dates and times and tell me where you were?"

Gammon didn't put names against the dates because of the first two murder that were not now being investigated, but he did still leave the times just to see what he could dig up.

"Yes, I can Mr Gammon. The first date and time I was travelling to see the Bishop in Derby. I arrived at his house around 8.30pm so I would have been in my car at that time and date."

"Would the Bishop confirm this?"

"Yes, I'm sure he would."

"What's his name, Andrew?"

"Maurice Smithson, he lives at Millington House, Allestree near Derby. This is his mobile number."

Gammon felt that this seemed a little rehearsed and organised.

"Ok DI Kiernan, if you wouldn't mind giving the Bishop a call please."

Kiernan left the room.

"Ok, and the second date?"

"I was preparing the church, we had a funeral the following day."

"Can anybody verify this?"

Able thought for a minute.

"Mrs Killeen from Bridge House, Brichover, she helps at the church."

"Do you have a number for Mrs Killeen?"

"Yes."

Able looked in his phone and wrote down the number.

"Ok Andrew, thank you. Now what about the next two?"

"Well that one," he said pointing to the time of Freeman Gillespie.

PAY FOR YOUR SIN

"I am guessing I would have been in bed, and the next one again in bed I guess."

"Ok Andrew, this may be unpleasant for you, but I have to ask these questions. You were jailed for sexual harassment?"

"That is correct Mr Gammon, but two things you need to know. I didn't do what they say I did and secondly I am a different man now."

"I don't doubt that Andrew, but the facts are you were convicted of the offence and you were incarcerated, were you not?"

Able stayed very calm, almost confident Gammon thought.

"Yes, that is correct."

"Now the name change. When you were a celebrity you called yourself Bobby King."

"That's correct."

"Why did you change your name from Ricky Peter Flag?"

"My agent suggested it. All celebrities do it, Mr Gammon."

"Do you miss that life that was taken away from you by the sexual harassment scandal and subsequent jail term?"

"No, I honestly don't miss it. I am happier now than I have ever been in my life."

"Ok, going back to your given name, Ricky Peter Flag, as you are aware our killer is killing people and carving the initials 'RPF' into the base of their foot. Funnily that is your initials Andrew, but then because you have changed your name twice, you wouldn't have been flagged up, would you?"

The solicitor broke into the conversation.

"What are you implying, DCI Gammon? That my client killed these people then marked their bodies with his initials. A little far-fetched, don't you think?"

"No, I wouldn't. You see each of these murders have been linked to the ten commandments, and whilst this isn't common knowledge who better than a vicar with a grudge to carry out these killings?"

"Mr Gammon, you have already convicted a man for two of the murders, are you saying he was convicted wrongly?"

Gammon didn't want this and knew it would go pear shape.

"What we believe we have, is a copycat killer, Mr Tuft."

"What a good get out, Mr Gammon. You see a man take his own life and you find that the killer is still at large, so now Bixton Police Station are saying it's a copycat killer. How convenient. To add insult to injury you try and get another innocent man involved in the murders because he had a record of sexual harassment and is now a vicar, so he would know about the Ten Commandments. I find this distasteful and arrogant of you and your force. I will be contacting our local MP and your Chief Constable. Now unless you have something more concrete we will end this now."

Gammon knew this would happen. Now the brown stuff was really going to hit the fan.

Tuft and Andrew Able had left when DI Kiernan came back.

"Sorry it's taken so long Sir, but only just located the Bishop. He did confirm Andrew Able had a meeting with him, but not until 12.20pm. It was originally scheduled before, but he couldn't make it. He wasn't sure if Able had set off."

"Ok, let's keep a note of that. You and Bass go to this address and see if a Mrs Killeen can back up his story please."

"Danny you might as well take DS Bass along as well."

"Ok Sir."

Next up was Alistair Mackay. Gammon didn't hold much out with this one though. Mackay was a tall guy, balding with glasses, slightly stooped and looked too old to have been involved in the killings. He refused a solicitor. DS Winnipeg set the tape going and Milton sat with Gammon.

"Good morning Mr Mackay, thank you for coming. May I call you Alistair?"

"You may," he said in a quivery voice.

"You may be wondering what this was about Alistair. Could you tell me your whereabouts for these times and dates please?"

Mackay felt into his coat pocket and produce a pair of glasses. He looked for a few minutes then said, "Yes."

"Ok, for the record, where were you?"

"I was in hospital for an operation on my gall bladder."

That just about killed the interview, but Gammon went through the motions.

"Who was the surgeon and which hospital, Alistair?"

"Micklock and the surgeons name was?"

"Wilson."

"Ok, we will need to confirm this Alistair, so we will take a break here."

"DS Winnipeg, get Alistair a drink while myself and DI Milton check this out."

Gammon got outside.

"He hardly looks killer material, Sir."

PAY FOR YOUR SIN

"Yes, I think this is a dead-end if it checks out."

Gammon rang the hospital and confirmed Alistair Mackay had been in for a gall bladder operation.

"That's it then, Carl. Thank him for his time and send him on his way."

"Will do, Sir."

Gammon went back to his office and within seconds DCI Rose had entered.

"The brown stuff has hit the fan. Chief Constable Sim wants to see both of us in Derby. The nationals have got hold of the story and potential cover up on the first two murders. Sounds serious, John."

"It will be, what it will be, Jenny. Let's go and see him and see which one he wants to throw under the bus, shall we?"

Sim wanted the meeting off site for obvious reasons and chose a small pub next to the river in Fairbrook. Sim said to be there at 1.00pm prompt. Gammon and Rose arrived, and they could see Andrew Sim sitting in the window. As they entered the pub Sim gestured for them to come over and take a seat.

They sat down, and Sim was quite amiable.

"Well you made a pig's ear of that this morning."

Gammon tried to defend himself, but Sim wasn't having any of it.

"Now what are you two going to do to get the force out of the mess you have put on it?"

Gammon was starting to feel angry.

"With the greatest of respect Sir, but you instructed me personally to let the first two murders stay with Tommy Spire."

"I think Gammon, you should be careful what you say to your superior officer."

John had the evidence so said no more.

PAY FOR YOUR SIN

"I realise this is a bad situation for you DCI Rose, so I will ask you to wait in the car while I discuss what Gammon needs to say to the press."

Jenny smiled at Gammon, but not so Sim could see her.

"Ok Gammon, I should have listened to everyone and known you were trouble. If you think I am taking the fall for this, you are mistaken. At 3.00pm today there will be a press conference which you and myself will attend. I will say you have something to say with regard to the perceived cover up of the first two murders. You will then take full responsibility for your actions. Are we clear Gammon?"

"Crystal, Sir."

"Well if you end up being booted out of the force I will put in for ill health retirement for you, so you keep your police pension etc."

"Thank you, Sir," Gammon said in a condescending voice.

"Be at the Majestic Club at 2.50pm. That's about an hour so you probably have time for a last supper," he said then laughed as he walked away. John called Jenny back in and bought some lunch before heading to the Majestic club. It was incredible the amount of vans with reporters from everywhere outside the Majestic.

John and Jenny made their way through what could only described as a pack of wolves chasing down a deer.

"Ok, DCI Rose you sit in the audience. I dare say after this I will be announcing you as overall DCI of Bixton station."

PAY FOR YOUR SIN

Jenny looked at John who seemed so calm, not one bit annoyed by Sim's arrogance,

Cameras were flashing as they took the stage. Sim stood up.

"Ladies and gentleman, things have been quite tough, and DCI Gammon has been involved from the start, so I will let him tell you where he feels the investigation went wrong. May I add before DCI Gammon speaks that I fully support him in his decision."

Gammon stood up.

"I was the investigating officer in the Annie Bird and Amy Lord case of which Tommy Spire was a prime suspect. He was charged, and a jury found him guilty. When Mr Spire took his own life we had another murder exactly the same as the others. A few days later at this point I started to have doubts, so I spoke with

Chief Constable Andrew Sim, and this was his reply."

Gammon pulled out his phone and laid it next to the microphone. The evidence was damming for Sim. The room was shocked. Sim looked at Gammon. Gammon sat down and quietly said, "Hope you keep your pension."

"What have you got to say Chief Constable? The way your police force is run you make poor decisions then expect other officers to take the fall for them?"

Sim got up red faced and left the room with thirty or forty cameras chasing after him.

Gammon was about to leave the stage when his phone rang. It was a gentleman called Graham Swann.

"Good afternoon DCI Gammon. I'm head of Her Majesty's Inspectorate of Constabulary and I have been instructed

PAY FOR YOUR SIN

by the Home office and Sir William
Colden to speak with you today with
regard to an article just played to him on
the case of a cover up at Bixton Police
Station in Derbyshire. Can you make your
way to The Holgate Hotel in Mayfair for
7.30pm? I would book a room on expenses
as it may be a long evening. I will instruct
the reception where I will be when you
arrive. Ok, I will see you at 7.30pm."

Gammon took DCI Rose back to Bixton,
nipped home and got a clean change of
clothes and headed for London. John was
unsure what to expect. Was this the end of
his career perhaps?

He arrived at the Holgate in Mayfair and
what a plush hotel it was. He booked in,
showered, changed and was down at
reception for 7.30pm. He spoke with the
Maître D who showed John to a table
where a well-dressed man in his early

forties was sitting. The man stood up and was about five feet eleven John thought.

"Graham Swann," he said thrusting out his hand for John to shake.

John reciprocated.

"Nice to meet you."

"Please take a seat. We shall have dinner then I need to discuss with you the way forward Mr Gammon."

Gammon took that to be positive. He ordered sardines escabche with celery and kohlrabi slaw and a black olive crumb. For the main he had tournedos of beef with a parmesan leek gratin and pomme gaufrette with a bordelaise jus.

They both finished their courses and Swann ordered them a double brandy each.

"Would you like dessert, John?"

This is going well Gammon thought.

"I would prefer cheese and biscuits."

PAY FOR YOUR SIN

Swann called over the waiter and ordered a cheese basket which was absolutely amazing when it arrived. John could eat but was feeling a little full now.

"Ok, so now down to business. The Home Office had for some time had concerns about Andrew Sim, John. What you did today, whilst I can't condone it, I do understand it."

"This is what we propose to do. You will get an increase of twenty two thousand pounds. You will stay as DCI at Bixton but will attend Derby headquarters twice a month as acting Chief Constable. How does that sound?"

"Sounds pretty good."

"We at the Home Office are well aware of your commitment and ability DCI Gammon, but what I will tell you is this time your maverick ways saved your job.

Be very careful in future how the maverick side of you comes out."

"What about Jenny Rose?"

"If you are ok with working alongside her then stay as you are. I hear she is good at your paperwork," which made John smile.

"Right John, I best get some shut eye. I have a meeting in Lima, Peru tomorrow night so a long flight ahead of me tomorrow. Thank you for coming."

"No, thank you, Sir."

Swann left, and John ordered another double brandy. Wow he thought, that turned out well.

The following morning John had the sumptuous breakfast before checking out. He reached for his credit card and would claim it back, but the girl said the account was settled by Graham Swann.

PAY FOR YOUR SIN

Going back up the motorway playing his favourite record 'The Night' by Frankie Vali, he could not believe how it had all turned out so good.

John arrived back at Bixton at 1.50pm and was met by Jenny Rose.

"Have you got a minute, John?"

"Yes of course, are you ok?"

"Well I am a bit concerned seeing that Sim put me in this job."

"Sit down, I have loads to tell you," and John went through what had happened with Graham Swann the night before.

"I have arranged for a small press conference just to put the record straight, Jenny. I think that is only right and proper I do that."

"I agree, John. So, we are still going to be working together then, John?"

"We certainly are Jenny. The 'A Team' eh?

The following day Gammon arranged the small press conference and the media boys all seemed to like what John had to say and it was as if they knew he was a straight copper.

"Ok Jenny, that went well. Now we need to get the killer."

Gammon called DI Kiernan to his office. He had been to see Mrs Killen the other person Andrew Able said would vouch for him.

"So, Mrs Killeen did she say she saw Able at the time and date he said?"

"Bit difficult that one, Sir. She is very confused. She has started with Alzheimer's and gets very confused."

"Buggar, so we really can't do much about that. We just have the bishop saying he didn't see Able until 12.30, but if Able had set off then he could have an alibi.

PAY FOR YOUR SIN

Let's save that one but I want twenty four hour surveillance on Able DI Kiernan."

"Ok sir, will get it set up now."

Almost three days passed with nothing untoward reported on Andrew Able, although Gammon was quite convinced he was the man.

He had left work when his phone rang. It was Saron.

"John, hi you ok?"

"Yes thanks, Saron."

"Oh, I wondered because not heard from you for a bit."

John felt confused; one minute he basically was getting the cold shoulder then the next Saron was all friendly.

"Look, I'm off tonight, do you fancy going bowling?"

John was taken back by this request but said yes all the same.

"I will pick you up at 7.30pm, if that's ok Saron?"

"Lovely John. I will be ready."

John arrived at the Tow'd Man spot on 7.30pm and Saron was waiting which was quite unusual. She was never on time.

John couldn't help but admire her figure. She had a pair of skin-tight, brown leather leggings with a bright orange top and short cropped cardigan.

"Evening, you look stunning as ever."

"Well thank you John, I try."

"Which bowling alley are we going to?"

"I thought Sparkies in Derby, so I booked that John, and I thought we could have a meal at Miriam's Cluster."

"Never heard of that place, Saron."

"It's new. Donna went there the other night with three of the locals and she said it was excellent."

"What food is it?"

PAY FOR YOUR SIN

"Bit of a mix, mainly Argentinian but they do some American apparently."

"Sounds great."

"We are last sitting at 9.00pm, John."

They arrived at the bowling alley and John found it highly amusing that Saron had to wear the bowling slippers.

"What's so funny, Gammon?"

"Sorry, just you look so stunning and those slippers don't really complement the outfit," and he laughed.

"Right for that I will beat you at this."

"We'll see."

The score ended up at 3-1 to Saron. John knew he would not hear the last of this as they entered the Argentinian restaurant. Miriam's Cluster had about forty covers and was quite intimate.

A dark-haired guy showed them to their table and introduced himself as Summal.

"I will be your waiter for the evening. Here are the menus. May I get you something to drink?"

"I'll have a passion fruit caipirinha please."

"And for you Sir?"

"A lychee margarita please."

"Coming right up. This is this evening's menu and the three dishes here are the chef's specials."

The waiter disappeared.

"John, this looks really good."

"Yes, I like it. The whole ambience of the place is good."

On the waiters return Saron ordered calamari fritti and John ordered the cuadril with veg.

They had almost finished when the waiter asked if they would like more calamari or steak.

"We are fine, thank you."

PAY FOR YOUR SIN

"But you must see our desert menu."

They agreed and the waiter brought it over.

"Oh, wow John, this isn't good for the figure."

"Like you need to worry," and he laughed.

"I will have the rogel cake please and could I have a strong black coffee at the same time?"

"For you Madam?"

"Can you recommend something?"

"My personal favourite is dulce de leche."

"Sounds wonderful and could I have an americano with my dessert."

"Of course," the waiter said in his accent.

"Anything for the pretty lady," which made Saron blush.

On the way home John turned to Saron.

"Did you enjoy that?"

"It was wonderful John, but."

"But what, Saron?"

"Oh nothing, it will keep."

John was now intrigued.

They arrived back at the Tow'd Man and Saron leaned over and kissed John on his cheek.

"Don't I get an invite in?"

"Not tonight Romeo," she said and left John crest-fallen as she disappeared down the steps into the pub.

John sat for what must have been a good five minutes trying to figure out what that was all about before heading home.

John lay in bed thinking. It was a clear night although quite cold, so he left the curtains open. He could see all the stars sparkling like cosmic flashlights in the sky. What was Saron about to say before she checked herself? It couldn't have been

PAY FOR YOUR SIN

anything bad because they had such a good time.

CHAPTER FIVE

The following day John arrived at work and Magic met him.

"Sir, got a scruffy looking guy, well he actually looks like a tramp. Di Trimble said he has been here all night he wants to speak with you."

"Where is he?"

"In Interview room two. I got him a coffee and a bacon sandwich. It doesn't look like he has eaten, Sir."

"Ok well done, Magic."

Gammon nipped to his office to drop his bag off and made his way down to the interview room.

The man, Gammon thought, was mid-forties but because he was sleeping rough he looked more like mid-sixties. He had long, straggly, blonde hair with a black beanie hat on, a long beard which had flecks of grey in it. His clothes were old and his jacket was too big on him.

The man had just finished his sandwich leaving a couple of pieces of bacon stuck in his beard.

"DCI John Gammon."

"I know who tha is Mr Gammon."

"And who are you?"

"Simon Bertrand Charles William Snow but everybody calls me Snowy."

"Can I call you Snowy?"

"That wanna be a problem, Mr Gammon."

"So Snowy, I believe you would like to talk to me. What about exactly?"

"Well you probably guessed I sleep rough. My family are the owners of Snow Mill in Puddle Dale."

"What the one that had been a cotton mill and is now converted to thirty six luxury flats?"

"Yes, that's correct."

"So, how come you sleep rough?"

"I fell out with my parents when I was twenty eight and never seen them since."

"So, you have been living on the streets ever since?"

"Not quite, the first two years I stayed at a friend's house, but we fell out so that's when I started sleeping rough."

"So where do you sleep?"

"I have made a small camp in Sparrow Dale, and before you saying anything I know it's illegal. I am at peace with myself up there and I do some work for Johnny Grainger who farms nearby, and his wife feeds me two meals a day."

"Look Snowy, I really have no interest in you breaking the law in Sparrow Dale, but I am intrigued what you want me for?"

PAY FOR YOUR SIN

"Well I keep myself to myself. I like it that way, but this has been playing on my mind."

"What exactly?"

"Well yesterday while I was having my lunch Mrs Grainger asked me if I had seen the Micklock Mercury and the article about the guy murdered up there who was a druid. I read the article and there was a picture of the guy and it said his name was Hayden Tusker. I recognised him because he was at Sparrow Dale, they congregate round the nine stones. I was walking past and this guy, the guy in the picture, asked me to join them. I declined. From nowhere another guy in white robes came over, and in a dialect I didn't understand, began arguing with that Tusker guy. I decided to move on quickly, I don't like confrontation, Mr Gammon. I wondered if he may have killed Tusker?"

"How many people were actually there at the time?"

"Not as many as usual, maybe eight or nine."

"What was the mix?"

"I would say probably six men including those two and three women, but I can't be one hundred percent sure."

"If I got a line up, would you be willing to pick out the man who was arguing with Tusker, Snowy?"

"I don't want no trouble, Mr Gammon."
"They won't be able to see you, Snowy. It's one-way glass. I would get an officer to pick you up and take you back."

"What if the police officer sees my camp at Sparrow Dale? Will he arrest me?"

"Rest assured Snowy, you will be fine."

"Ok, I will do it then. Do you know Sparrow Dale?"

"Yes, quite well actually."

PAY FOR YOUR SIN

"Well get on Sparrow Moor, head for the nine ladies and there is a tight path that takes you down to Sparrow Dale. Half way down there is an overgrown path. Walk about a third of a mile and look to your right. You won't be able to see the camp, but I will see you or your officer and I will make my way out to you."

"Appreciate that Snowy, we will be in touch."

Gammon collared DI Kiernan and DS Bass and told them to find the local druid club that Tusker was involved in. Then to arrange for the male members to come in for a line up. Gammon got DCI Rose up to speed on Snowy.

"You seem quiet Jenny, you ok?"

"Yeah fine John. I may have to take about a month off. My mother hasn't been well back home, so I feel I should do my bit, if you know what I mean."

"Hey, of course Jenny, just be prepared to come back to a mountain of paperwork to deal with."

"Wouldn't expect anything else, John," she said laughing as she left his office.

Could snowy have seen the killer? It was a distinct possibility Gammon thought.

It was almost 4.00pm when a report came in that an office cleaner at an IT company had found a man stooped in his chair covered in blood. Gammon raced Wally and the team over and Smarty, Lee and he followed in two cars.

Magic Bubble was an IT Media company with offices on the way into Micklock. There were only three employees, all share-holders. Two of the guys were in London at a convention leaving just Charlie Stone actually in work.

PAY FOR YOUR SIN

They arrived and Wally got to work with his team. The cleaner, a lady in her late forties, was badly shaken. She was clearly a heavy smoker. Her whole being smelt of raw tobacco and her face very heavily wrinkled confirmed it.

Gammon showed his warrant card.

"You are the lady that found the body?"

"Yes."

"Your name please?"

"Sarah Tuffnell."

"Just run through how you came across the body."

"Could I smoke please?" she said lighting a cigarette with heavily stained nicotine fingers on her right hand.

"Feel free Sarah, you are in shock."

"I got to the office about 4.30pm and the door was unlocked so I went in. I called out to Mr Stone but I got no answer, so I assumed he was busy. I started to clean downstairs. I finished then went upstairs and that's when I found him."

Sarah started to cry sucking heavily on the remnants of her cigarette.

"Did you see anyone at all before you found the body of Mr Stone?"

Sarah looked puzzled.

"That's not Mr Stone. I don't know who he is, Mr Gammon."

"Ok look, I will get DI Lee to run you home. Here's my card if you think of anything, anything at all, please call me."

DI Lee took Sarah Tuffnell home and Gammon wandered over to Wally.

"What we got mate?"

"White male approximately six feet in height, killed in the same way, with his right foot scarred with the letters 'RPF', John."

"Great, that's all I need Wally. Full results for 9.00am tomorrow mate please."

PAY FOR YOUR SIN

"Will do John," and Wally went back to his team.

It was almost 5.30pm when Gammon's phone rang. It was PC Magic.

"Sir, just had the owner of Chrichton Cars in Micklock on. He said his sales guy left with a customer at lunch time in a new Ford Focus RS and hasn't returned."

"Ok Magic, tell him I am on my way."

What the hell was this all about he thought as he drove the ten minutes into Micklock and Crichton Cars.

Gammon knew the car sales place. His dad always insisted in buying his mum's car from them when she was alive. His dad had been at school with Harvey Crichton and he said he always gave him a good deal, although Gammon doubted it knowing car salesmen. Harvey Crichton was a distinguished gentleman, old school you might say.

"Good evening Sir, DCI Gammon," and he produced his warrant card.

"I believe you are concerned about one of your sales persons."

"Are you Philip Gammon's lad?"

"Yes, I am."

"Well blow me down. I was sorry to hear he had passed away. Always bought your Mum's cars from me, did Philip."

Typical salesman John thought, more interested in a sale than a friendship.

"So, can you just run through the problem, Mr Crichton?"

"Harvey lad, call me Harvey."

"Ok Harvey."

"Well, I had a golfing tournament in Derby, so there was only my secretary Amelia and Richard in. Richard took a client out for a test drive and hasn't returned."

"Is that Richard Honeywell?"

PAY FOR YOUR SIN

John pointed to a picture in the foyer.

"Yes, grand lad and a good salesman, Richard."

Gammon knew instantly that the body he had seen was Honeywell's.

"Ok Harvey, have you got the number plate of the vehicle? I can get my police officers looking for it and Mr Honeywell."

Harvey Crichton fumbled about in the reception. Gammon could see this guy wasn't on site much.

"There you go."

Crichton handed Gammon the car registration.

"Ok Harvey, I will let you know, but quite often these things are pinched and never seen again, but you never know."

"Ok give me a call when you have something."

Gammon got back in his car thinking how cold Harvey Crichton had been. He

never mentioned Richard Honeywell. He
was more concerned with a stupid car.
Strange world we live in he thought. John
picked up his mobile to phone Jenny Rose
to let her know about Honeywell, but
stopped short Jenny had gone back to look
after her mother for a month. You are on
your own lad he thought.

It was now almost 8.00pm so John
thought he would call and see how the new
landlord and landlady at the Spinning
Jenny were doing. Wez was behind the bar
stocking the bottles and Lyndsay was
bringing out food for a table of four.

"Hey John, good to see you."

"Thanks Lyndsay, how are you doing?"

"Loving it, we are so lucky to have such
lovely regulars. Wez has been golfing with
Bob, Cheryl's husband. I didn't know he
was a comedian, John?"

PAY FOR YOUR SIN

"Oh, he is very popular, is Pants On Yer Head Bob."

"Is that what he calls himself, why?"

"It's all to do with when he started doing it. For a laugh, women used to throw their knickers at him, you know, like they did at Tom Jones years ago. Before my time I'm afraid John. Well anyway Bob stuck a pair on his head for a laugh and the act was born."

"What can I get you, John?"

"I'll have a Pedigree please, Wez."

Lyndsay went back in the kitchen and John stood talking to Wez.

"You a football fan, John?"

"I used to like playing, still watch England games and Match of the Day if I get time. Why?"

"Well I've got a spare ticket for Villa versus Spurs in the FA Cup, if you fancy?"

"Thanks mate, but I'm United through and through."

"Who? Leeds United?"

"Don't be naughty or I will arrest you," and John laughed.

"Anyway, what is a Barnsley lad doing being a Villa fan?"

"You can blame my dad for that."

"Making you follow the Villa, that's tantamount to child abuse, mate."

"Certainly has been over the last few years, John."

It was almost 9.00pm and John was thinking of calling it a night when Jack and Bob with Kev came in.

"Hey, what you motley crew up to?"

"Phil just dropped us off. He is picking Shelley, Cheryl, Sheba and Doreen up from Badminton at Pritwich village hall."

"So, you lot been out then?"

PAY FOR YOUR SIN

"Yeah, we had a ride up to the Star at Puddle Dale. Very busy John, but your mate doesn't look to happy with life. He is very brown though from his honeymoon."

"I didn't know he was back yet."

John was thinking that maybe India had contacted him. He shuddered at the thought things might get out about him and India. It wasn't a fear thing more a thought he might lose his best mate's friendship.

They had almost finished their first drink when the girls arrived.

"Enjoying retirement, Doreen?"

"Loving it John, so nice to have our lives back. Don't get me wrong, had some wonderful years, but this is great isn't it, Kev?"

"Yes, my dear, love it."

"Blimey John, how long is this winter going to go on? It had started to snow again as we left Pritwich."

"If it carries on snowing Puddle Dale will be cut off, Cheryl."

"Yes, it's always been open to the elements and where Steve is at the Star that always gets cut off."

"Remember my dad saying in the bad snowfall in nineteen fourty seven that Puddle Dale was cut off for almost three weeks. It was only the pub that kept everyone fed and watered, John."

"Hey, anybody up for Jacks?"

"Are you sure, Shelley?"

"I was telling Wez about it and he said next time we are all together he will join in."

"What do you reckon, Mr Sterndale?"

"Never played it Sheba, but always up for something new."

PAY FOR YOUR SIN

"Get a glass, Wez."

"Coming up, John."

"Ok Wez and Phil, seeing that it's your first time these are the rules. The cards don't get shuffled. The first Jack out names a drink, the second Jack out names a drink, the third Jack pays for the two drinks, and the fourth Jack has to drink it in one. If they don't they have to pay for a round of drinks for the other players. Oh and the same glass is used throughout the game. We deal anti-clock-wise, so I'll start, Sheba next etc etc."

John got the first Jack to howls of cheat from Phil Sterndale. Jack got the next Jack, so now there was brandy and gin in the glass. The next Jack out fell to Cheryl.

"Looks like you are paying, Cheryl."

"You mean Bob is, John."

"She is like the bloody Queen, she never carries money."

"That's what I married you for Bob," and she laughed.

John was almost at the bottom of the pack before the final Jack came out, and it fell on Wez. The whole table erupted in laughter. Poor Wez's face as he downed the concoction was a sight to see.

By 11.00 am Doreen was asleep on Kev having had to drink 6 drinks. Cheryl was slumped on Bob, she had five drinks. Wez had three drinks and being a big lad it didn't seem to have much effect on him. Jack was slurring, having had eight of the drinks. Nobody else, other than Sheba who had to drink one, had won the drink Jack.

"Great game John, I paid for seven drinks and never won one."

"You got your money's worth Kev, look at Doreen."

"So, I spent a fortune, I have to get Doreen home in this state and I got my monies worth! Are you having a laugh, mate?"

The following morning John showered and headed into work ready for the 9.00am meeting in the incident room and hopefully a break through from Wally's team. The roads were quite bad on his way to Bixton, to the point he wondered if he would make it.

He arrived at the station and only DI Kiernan had failed to show so Gammon was quite pleased with that. They assembled in the incident room and Gammon asked Wally to talk through what he had.

"The dead man was a white male, his dental records show his name is Richard Honeywell of number three, Stinton View, Micklock. He had his throat cut and on the base of his right foot was our serial killer's markings 'RPF'."

"Any DNA from our killer, Wally?"

"Yes, we did find a very small amount but as yet nothing is showing up on any data base."

"Ok, DI Smarty and DI Lee, let's trawl our data base. I want to know everything about this guy even down to the colour of his underpants."

"Ok Sir," they replied.

"DS Yap, you and DS Bass check his bank accounts for any irregularities."

"Ok Sir."

"DI Milton and DS Winnipeg, you do some door to door. Let's see what made this guy tick. I am looking at who his friends were, what he did socially, all that sort of stuff?"

"Everyone back here same time tomorrow."

PAY FOR YOUR SIN

"Oh Carl, get the traffic lads out looking for this Ford car," and he handed him the number plate.

"If we find it, get it towed back here and hand it over to Wally's team to crawl over. I will go and see his widow. Thanks."

Gammon left for Honeywell's house. He arrived at number three, Stinton View, a neat detached house in a cul-de-sac of six houses. Gammon knocked on the door and a woman in her mid-forties opened it. A big Alsatian started barking at Gammon.

"Stop it, Merlot," she said the dog stopped immediately.

"Very impressed. Are you Mrs Honeywell?" and Gammon showed his warrant card.

"Yes, what's the problem?"

"May I step inside?"

"Oh yes, sorry please excuse the mess. I only got back this morning. Been to see my sister in Hastings and typical man, my husband John, hasn't tidied up."

"It's actually about your husband is the reason I am here, Mrs Honeywell."

"Why, whatever is a matter? Has he been involved in an accident?"

"No, I am very sorry to tell you but your husband was found dead yesterday in Micklock."

Mrs Honeywell started to cry. Gammon got her a glass of water.

"Have you anybody you can call? Have you any children?"

"No," she said in a muffled tone.

"Richard couldn't, oh it doesn't matter now, does it?" and she sobbed some more.

"What happened?"

"I'm afraid whoever killed him took him to an IT company and the cleaner found him. His throat had been cut. Did he have any regular friends? Was he a member of any clubs?"

"He was the manager of Rowksly 46. He played for them for many years and then took on the manager's job. He lived for his football, Mr Gammon. Can I call my sister-in-law? She will come round."

Mrs Honeywell called a number and told the lady to come round straight away as she needed to talk.

"Mrs Honeywell, I do need you to come to the mortuary to positively identify the victim."

She nodded her head. Honeywell's sister in law arrived so Gammon left and decided to head for Rowksly to see if he could tie any loose ends up. Rowksly football club was a neat ground, and a guy was marking out the pitch, so Gammon wandered over.

"Good morning Sir, I'm DCI John Gammon."

"Waggy, nice to meet you. Are you a Rowksly fan?"

"No, Mr Waggy."

"I'm just Waggy, been part of this club man and boy, Mr Gammon. You should come down and watch us."

"I just might do that, Waggy."

"I'm afraid I have some bad news for you, Waggy. Richard Honeywell was found murdered last night."

Waggy's face went ashen.

"What! Me and Richard have run this and the reserves for many years. What happened?"

"I'm afraid I can't go into detail, but he was murdered."

"Who the hell would murder Rich? I can't believe it. Do you know when he played he was the best midfielder around.

PAY FOR YOUR SIN

In fact Derby looked at him, but he was twenty four years old by then, so their interest disappeared. He could have easily made it to the top level, Mr Gammon. Blimey, this has really shocked me. Have you time for a cuppa?"

"That would be good, Waggy."

Waggy opened the door to the wooden club house painted green with the Rowksly 46 logo over the door saying 'We Are Rowksly 46' proudly positioned for all to see.

Waggy made two strong cups of tea and insisted Gammon had a Jammie Dodger. He said they were Richard Honeywell's favourite.

"What can you tell me about Richard? I need some background, Waggy."

"Well, he was a normal guy. We were at school together and he got a job cleaning cars for Chrichton Cars in Micklock.

When he left school at seventeen they offered him a trainee salesman's job. But Richard being Richard, said he would only take it if he could finish at lunch on Saturday during the football season. They agreed so we played together for Tidza Blue Star, a top team at the time. My mum and dad used to take us everywhere. Richard was quite a shy lad off the pitch when he was younger, but a flippin' master on it."

"Is that him there, Waggy?"

"Yes, we had just won the Derbyshire Cup with Rowksly. That was the night he asked his missus to marry him. Think we were twenty three in that picture. We have won it seven times, you know," Waggy said proudly.

All the time John was listening to Waggy he was thinking how lucky Waggy was, having something in his life he cared so much about. Gammon had decided he would pop up and watch a game with Waggy. He liked the guy and his honesty.

"Another Jammie, Mr Gammon?"

"No, I best get back. I will give you my card, if you think of anything that could relate to Richard's death then call me please."

"I will and thanks for the natter, that came as a blow, Mr Gammon."

"See you Waggy and I will get up for a match."

"You do that, Mr Gammon."

Gammon left Rowksly and headed for Bixton. It was almost 4.10pm when he got back in his office and he decided that the paperwork wouldn't wait for Jenny Rose to come back. He thought it best to work his way through it. First though he needed to check his e-mails. John's heart

gladdened, the first e-mail was from Fleur
Dubois.

'Hi John, sorry I haven't been in touch
things have been quite hectic. How are
things in your life? I can't see me getting
anytime off until at least August, so save
some days and we can meet up,
Congratulations on being a DCI it's well
deserved. Speak soon Fleur.'

John felt elated she had been in touch.
He worked his way down his e-mails.
Although he had never given Anouska his
e-mail address there was one from her.

'Dear John, hope this e-mail finds you
well. I am sorry for the mess I created last
time I came over but I wondered if you
wanted to come and stop with me and your
daughter for a week next week. Let me
know Anouska xxx'

Bloody hell, it's one of those days, but as
much as he would like to go and see his

daughter, he had too much going on at work.

It was now 7.10pm and John called for a Chinese take-away, his usual Singapore chow mein, extra hot, egg fried rice and onion rings He never finished it all in one night, so it would probably make two meals he thought as he portioned it up.

He watched a program on George Best, his hero, and again thought how committed and involved Waggy was. Poor Richard Honeywell would no longer enjoy the enthusiasm they both shared for Rowksly 46.

The following day as agreed they all met in the incident room.

"Sir, had a bloke call in, said he has been trying to contact you. He said to say it was Waggy and could he meet you at Libby's tea room in Rowksly at 11.00am today?"

John looked at his mobile and it was dead. Damn thing he thought, the battery must be on its way out.

"Ok thanks, Magic."

"Ok everyone, what have we got? DS Bass?"

"Well his bank accounts on the face of it were normal. Then we went back three years where he paid out twelve thousand pounds, and guess what the recipient's initials were? Only RF."

"Have we managed to trace RF?"

"Not yet Sir, but we are looking."

"Ok DS Bass, good work."

DS Bass sat down beaming. She felt she was part of the team now.

"DS Winnipeg, anything from you and DI Milton on the door to door?"

"No Sir, we drew a blank."

"Ok DI Smarty and DI Lee, anything?"

PAY FOR YOUR SIN

"Yes, we found that Mr Honeywell took a neighbour to court five years ago. He won his case but two years back the neighbour committed suicide."

"What was his name?"

"Jack Fernley."

"And what was the case?"

"Apparently, it had been going on for a while. Jack Fernley had bought a car from Chrichton Cars in Micklock where Honeywell worked, and Fernley had the car back five times with an engine fault. In court Honeywell said that Mr Chrichton offered to give Mr Fernley a new car after the third complaint, but Fernley refused. The judge said that Chrichton Cars had acted correctly and came down on the side of Chrichton Cars. Three years after the case he was found dead in his garage by his brother Rick. There was a suicide letter stating that Honeywell had lied in court.

Fernley was a religious man he said his neighbour had born false witness against him."

"So, we have a brother with the initials RF and a possible motive, Sir. Revenge for his brother's death perhaps?"

"Right I want everyone on this. Let's find this Rick Fernley."

"As soon as he is located I want him in here for questioning. Ok everyone, get to it."

Gammon left for the meeting with Waggy at 11.00am.

Gammon headed for Libby's tea room in Rowksly. It was a quaint little tea room legend that Queen Victoria and Prince Albert once took afternoon tea there on their way to Chatsworth House. There was no evidence to support this, but subsequent owners had used the legend to get punters

in, and it worked. The place was full but
Waggy had a seat by the bow window.

"Waggy, how are you mate?"

"Good, Mr Gammon."

"John, call me John, Waggy."

"Ok John. I've ordered us both a home-
made toasted teacake when I saw you pull
up. They are the best, mate. You have to
try one."

The tea cakes arrived with a pot of tea
and pot of hot water, all very nice.

"So Waggy, you thought of something?"

"Look, if it helps find Richard's killer I
will tell you what he told me in
confidence. Richard Honeywell was a very
honest, decent man but that guy he worked
for, Harvey Chrichton, was the opposite.
Richard told me he had lied in court over a
guy who had a grievance with Chrichton
Cars. He said he had no choice. Harvey
Chrichton had told him if he didn't lie for

him he would lose his job and the sponsorship of Rowksly. To be honest I don't think it was about losing his job. He loved the football club and he knew we needed that sponsorship."

"Why did he tell you, Waggy?"

"Like I said John we were like brothers, and when that guy committed suicide I think he had to tell someone what he had done. He was beside himself John."

"Well that answers a few questions, Waggy."

"I just hope it helps you get his killer, John. Big match this Saturday, we've got Swinster Celtic in the Dilley Dale Cup. You coming to watch?"

"Loved to mate, but a lot on this week. I will see how it goes though."

"Kick -off is 3.00pm at Rowksly, John."

"Ok mate, and thanks for the info. I'm sure it will help."

PAY FOR YOUR SIN

"I hope so."

Gammon left Waggy finishing his tea cake looking like a contented Pooh Bear when he has honey.

Gammon decided to call at Dilley Dale and see Jeannette. He hadn't seen her in a long time and she was a good friend.

Sometimes in life fate takes a hand and this was to be one of those days. Jeannette was rushing about as normal and said she would meet him in Cheryl and Jackie's café, Make My Cake.

"Hey John, how are you?"

"I'm good Jackie."

"What did you do to Cheryl the other night? She never learns, playing Jacks with you lot. She was as rough has a bear. Bob brought her to work and she gone for a dental appointment today, so I am on my own."

"What can I get you?"

"A strong black coffee please, Jackie."

"What about a piece of trifle cake or our homemade sausage rolls?"

"No, I'm ok thanks Jackie, just had a tea cake at Libby's Tea Room in Rowksly."

"You flippin' traitor, John Gammon," and she laughed.

John sat down, and Jeanette came in and ordered a glass of water.

"Hello John, this is a pleasure."

"Sorry I've not been in touch, so much happening at work and then Steve getting married."

"I know John, that surprised me so soon after Jo."

"Yes, think most people were surprised but that's life, Jeannette. You just have to play with the card's you are dealt I guess."

"Terrible thing, that murder of Richard Honeywell. Him and his wife often called for an ice cream on a Sunday, never Saturday because of his football."

"What kind of man was he?"

"Very kind, very considerate would help anyone. I know when Rick Fernley had a go at him here one Sunday he was devastated. He blamed Richard for his brother's suicide, he said Richard lied in court. I had to ask Rick Fernley to leave."

"Do you know where he lives, Jeanette?"

"I believe he is the bar manager at that new wine bar in Micklock. I can't think what it's called."

"Jackie, what's that new wine bar called in Micklock?"

"Tuffins, why?"

"Was just telling John what a nice place it was."

John could not believe his luck. He thanked Jeanette for the company and called DI Smarty at the station to get down to Tuffins and get Rick Fernley in for questioning.

It was almost 3.00pm when Gammon got back to the Station. Smarty had Rick Fernley and his solicitor in interview room one.

Fernley was a suave character, well dressed and certainly didn't look like a killer. But you never know Gammon thought.

"Mr Fernley, I'm DCI Gammon. This is DI Smarty and DI Lee is operating the recording of this meeting."

"What the hell is this all about?"

"Am I correct in saying you were the brother of Jack Fernley?"

"Yes, Jack was my eldest brother."

"Do you have other brothers and sisters?"

"Yes, my younger brother Caleb, and my sister Natasha."

PAY FOR YOUR SIN

"Ok, I believe you had a grudge against Richard Honeywell."

"Oh, I get it now, you want to pin his murder on me?"

"I don't want to pin a murder on anybody if they weren't involved, but you have history Mr Fernley."

"Look my brother was stitched up by Honeywell and Crichton. I know it and the whole bloody world knows it. So, if some maniac decides to kill Honeywell, he has done me and my family a favour."

"Can you explain where you were on this date?"

Gammon pushed a date across to Fernley which was the date the cleaner found Honeywell's body.

"It was my day off from the wine bar, so I was chilling at home. That evening I went with my girlfriend to see 'Long way Home', the latest Jack Nicholson film."

"So, you have no alibi for the hours that we believe Richard Honeywell was murdered."

"I guess not," Fernley said all assured.

"What's your girlfriends name?"

"Karen Tuffnell."

"Any relation to Sarah Tuffnell?"

"Yes, they are sisters."

"Well that's interesting. And let me guess. Karen Tuffnell owns the wine bar you are the manager of?"

"So, what is wrong with that?"

"Nothing wrong with it, but what I will say is, you are my prime suspect in the murder of Richard Honeywell. You have a motive, you were seen arguing with the guy, and you don't have an alibi that can be substantiated by anyone for the hours leading up to Mr Honeywell's death. So, at present I have no reason to carry on questioning you."

PAY FOR YOUR SIN

"DI Smarty will take a DNA test for our records."

"I'm not sure my client needs to do this, Mr Gammon."

"Mr Brown, we have six murders on our hands. Whoever killed Richard Honeywell left DNA, so this isn't a request, it's an order."

"When DI Smarty has sorted the DNA test you are free to leave, but do not leave the country. We will be speaking again as this case progresses. Good day, Mr Fernley."

Fernley looked shocked as he left the interview room. It was either guilt that he had been rumbled, or the realisation that he was in it up to his neck Gammon thought.

"Dave, get everything you can on Karen Tuffnell. I want her business report from Company's House, her bank accounts, looking at in depth. Get Bass and Winnipeg helping you."

Gammon felt he may have had a small break through. Gammon had just sat at his desk when his phone rang.

"Hi Steve, how are you mate?"

"John, I need to talk to you. Can we meet for a beer tonight?"

"Of course mate, what time?"

"You can come straight from work?"

"Where do you want to meet?"

"I would prefer The Chicken Foot Tap House at Toad Holes, if you don't mind mate?"

"No, that's fine Steve, should be there at 5.45pm, if I get away on time?"

"Ok John, see you then," and Steve hung up.

Gammon stood looking over towards Losehill wondering what this was about, but he had an idea that maybe India had contacted John.

It took Gammon most of the day to finish his paperwork then he headed out to Toad Holes.

John arrived at the Chicken Foot Tap House. Steve was already there sitting by the bar. He didn't look himself.

"What are you drinking, John?"

"I'll try one of their micro beers."

"How about a Buffalo Soldier?"

"That will do mate."

"So, how are you mate?"

That's when Steve blurted it out.

"I've made a mistake, mate."

"What do you mean?"

"Marrying Imogen."

"What the hell, Steve? It's only been a couple of weeks. What's the problem?"

"India Green is the problem, John."

John could feel a well of concern running through him.

"She contacted me, and we met at the coffee house in Hittington. I was early, so ordered a coffee and was just taking a sip when she walked in. John, I honestly thought it was Jo. I almost dropped my coffee cup. She came and sat with me. She has the same mannerisms, although her eyes are the same colour, her left eye is slightly off colour. But it makes her so attractive. We sat and chatted for almost two hours. She doesn't want anything John. She just wanted to know about Jo and how we met etc."

"Have you told Tracey?"

"No, not yet John. I don't know what to do, but I can't get her out of my mind. She said she has a cottage she is renting because she writes books."

PAY FOR YOUR SIN

John was so hoping that Steve never found out about his dalliance with India on Christmas day. He knew even now he was besotted with her.

"So, what are you going to do?"

"I think I am going to contact her or go and see her. But I feel such an eel to Imogen, she has such big plans for us at the pub."

"Steve, you have to do what you think is best for the future."

"I realise now what you tried to do telling me about India before I got married, you were giving me the chance to walk away, weren't you?"

"Well I would be lying if I said it hadn't crossed my mind, Steve."

"Why am I so pig headed? So many people said it was too early after Jo, but would I listen?"

"Look mate, we all make mistakes, and boy, I have made plenty but do what you think is right for you. The trauma you had losing Jo and the little one was bound to wobble you. It would anybody, but I am here for you."

Steve went to get them another pint and John contemplated telling him about Christmas Day with India. But would that end their friendship and he could not take that chance, so he left it in the past, well at least for now.

Steve came back.

"Do you know mate, I feel so much better after talking to you. I am going to contact India tomorrow. Imogen is on a brewery course for two days."

They sat generally chatting when a tall guy with dark rimmed glasses dressed in a suit came over.

PAY FOR YOUR SIN

"Bloody hell, Porky Gammon and Offside, what you doing down here?"

Steve and John looked at the guy, with no idea who it was.

"Do you not remember me?"

John looked at Steve and in unison they both said, "No."

"Ady Grimshaw."

"What, Pip Squeak?"

"The very same."

"Bloody hell, you've grown, you must be six feet three?"

"Yep, and I was just short of five feet when I left in the second year at the big school."

"You went to live in Essex, didn't you?"

"Yeah, my dad was a biochemist and his job moved him down there."

"So, what brings you back?"

"I work for a beer seller. It's my job to go round the country trying out microbreweries, and if they are good we buy from them and deliver all over the country. I couldn't believe my luck when my boss sent me up here to Toad Holes."

"So, what do you reckon then, Ady?"

"Oh, this is a definite winner mate."

"So, how did you two do in your lives so far?"

"Here mate, grab a chair."

John pulled up a chair for Ady.

"Well I'm a DCI at Bixton."

"Oh wow, well done John. You didn't go into farming then?"

"No mate."

"Your brother liked farming if I remember?"

"Yeah, but afraid I lost my brother and mum and dad."

"Oh, I am sorry mate. What about you Steve?"

PAY FOR YOUR SIN

"Oh, I was in the Navy for some years. When I came out I met somebody, and we had a child together, but I lost them both I'm afraid. Just remarried Imogen Elliot. Can you remember her at school?"

"Yes, her parents ran the Star Inn in Puddle Dale. I heard she had done well for herself."

"Yes, she did but now she runs The Star."

"Well listen lads, got a taxi taking me to the station so will have to catch up again. I will call at the Star and we can all meet up. It's been great seeing you both."

"Same for us, Ady," John said.

"Well mate we best call it a night I guess."

"Thanks John, you are a good mate. I will let you know how I get on with India."

They both left and now it was John that was feeling under pressure. His only hope was India would not divulge anything. He didn't want to contact her, although in reality he had done nothing wrong. He was sure Steve would not think that way.

John arrived back home it was Phyllis Swan's cleaning day and she had left John a home-made meat and potato pie. John put a generous slice in the microwave and pored himself a large Jameson's.

John sat by his window looking down his garden at a rabbit and a small fox scurrying around. John finished his pie and poured another large Jameson before checking his e-mail. There was another e-mail from Anouska which was quite abrupt.

'John you don't even reply to me. Do you not want to see your daughter?'

PAY FOR YOUR SIN

It hurt John, but it was best he cut ties if he wanted any hope of getting back with Saron. He squared it in his mind that as long as he supported Anouska and the baby then he was ok.

It was almost midnight and John called it a night.

CHAPTER SIX

The following morning he was almost at Bixton when his phone vibrated.

"Hello."

"Sir, there has been another attack, only this time the man survived."

"Where is he, Magic?"

"Bixton General. DI Smarty and Milton are over there now, Sir."

"Ok, I'm on my way Magic, thanks."

Gammon arrived at the hospital and found Smarty and Milton on the third floor. There were a couple of nurses seeing to the young man.

"They said we could talk to him in a few minutes, Sir."

"Ok Carl, great. Who called the incident in?"

"It was a man. He wouldn't give his name, he just said he survived."

PAY FOR YOUR SIN

The nurses called the officers in.

"Five minutes please, he has had a traumatic time."

"Ok, thank you," Gammon said.

"Ok young man, what can you remember about the attack?"

"Well I had been cleaning the windows at 37 Horsedale View. And the lady there is, well you know, a bit hot."

"Hot?"

"Yeah, she flirts with me. Its harmless fun but if I took her up on it I'm sure it could go further. Anyway, I was having a coffee with her when there was a knock at the kitchen door. Mrs Lewis stood up. She had a really small skirt on and a low cut top and she answered the door."

"The man said he was a Jehovah's Witness. I didn't see his face because I had my back to him. Anyway, she said she wasn't interested. The man asked if she was married? She said yes. The man said maybe he could speak to her husband. She said he works away. Then he asked who I was? She said the window cleaner and to push off, because it was none of his business. She slammed the door in his face. I said I had to go as I had one more call before it got too dark. As I left she kissed me full on the lips."

"I took my ladders down an alleyway to get to the next house and that's when he hit me. He started saying I was coveting another man's wife. My head was spinning but he hit me again. I kept coming in and out of consciousness. I could see this bloody great knife and the pain in my foot. Next thing I know I wake up here. They said a man disturbed him."

"Did you get a glimpse of the man?"

"Only thing I can remember is he had ginger hair, but that's all."

PAY FOR YOUR SIN

"So, what's your name?"

"Martyn Bloom. Do you think it was the guy who came to Mrs Lewis's house?"

"Quite possibly Mr Bloom. Get some rest we may need to talk some more."

Gammon noticed the killer had carved 'RP' and part of another letter into the man's foot before he was disturbed.

"Ok Smarty, you come with me. We need to get a full identification of our Jehovah's Witness from Mrs Lewis."

Gammon and Smart headed for 37 Horsedale View. It was a detached house in a nice area. Gammon rang the doorbell and a woman in her early forties answered. They could see what Bloom meant about the provocative clothes Mrs Lewis was wearing. She immediately started flirting with Gammon before he introduced himself.

After their warrants were shown, she let them in the house.

"Ok Mrs Lewis, Martyn Bloom your window cleaner was attacked last night. He told us that whilst he was having a coffee with you here in the kitchen that a Jehovah's Witness came to your door, is that correct?"

"Yes, I told him I wasn't interested. When he saw Martyn he asked if my husband would be interested? I said he worked away, and he asked who Martyn was? I told him it was none of his business and to shove off.

"Ok, can you describe the man to me?

"He was about your height. Ginger hair, not particularly good looking like you, Inspector Gammon," and she re-arranged her blouse seductively.

"Would you recognise the man from a line up?"

PAY FOR YOUR SIN

"Definitely, I have a good memory for men."

Smarty smiled at that.

"Ok Mrs Lewis, we will be in touch."

Gammon and Smarty headed back to the station.

"Dave, I want everyone looking into any local Jehovah's Witness societies in the area. I believe there is a Kingdom Hall in Micklock and one in Ackbourne. Start there we need to find this man and quickly."

They entered the station and PC Magic said he had a call from a Graham Swann and could he phone him back.

"Damn, that's all I need."

Gammon went to his office and called Swann.

"Good morning, John."

"Good morning, Sir."

"So John, a little birdy tells me you still call yourself DCI Gammon, not acting Chief Constable, is that correct?"

"Yes sir, it doesn't feel right, unless the service decide I am actually the full-blown Chief Constable, not acting."

Swann went quiet at Gammons reply. After a brief pause he spoke again.

"Strange stand point John, anyway that isn't why I have called. As you can imagine the press boys are getting tetchy about the serial killer still not found. Where are we John?"

"We have a prime suspect, Sir. He attacked a man yesterday but was disturbed before he killed him. We now have identification and we believe we know who the man is. We just have to locate him."

"Ok John, well I am having a little party at my home to celebrate thirty five years of marriage to my wife, Marilyn. I would like you and your wife to attend."

"I'm.."

Before Gammon could say not married Swann said he wouldn't take no for an answer. He would see him Saturday night at 7.00pm at Clareston Lodge in Oxford. He said he would e-mail the full address later. Swann hung up.

"That's all I need, some posh party without a wife to take."

Gammon rang Saron and explained.

"Any chance you can get Saturday night off and come with me."

"Yes, I think so. What kind of party is it?"

John explained, and she said she would wear a nice dress. John felt better. He knew Saron would look a million dollars that was never going to be in question.

Gammon called a meeting to run through the case so far.

"Ok everybody, this is what we have," pointing to the victim board.

"Victim One, Amy Lord, husband found her. Do we have any background on this woman?"

"Yes, DI Milton."

"It appears she had been having an affair with a Thomas Muggles for some years."

"Have we contacted Mr Muggles to discount him from our enquiries?"

"I'm afraid he passed away over a year ago."

"Ok, victim two, Annie Board, found dead in the sheltered accommodation and previously been visited by a man she said his name was Dick. We got a description? Did it fit anything we have?"

"Yes, DS Bass?"

PAY FOR YOUR SIN

"Sorry sir, it was a blind alley, but we are still looking."

"Victim three, Freeman Gillespie. DI Lee?"

"Nothing on this guy, he was well liked, ran his business seven days a week no obvious reason why he was chosen."

"Victim four, Hayden Tusker. What have you got DS Winnipeg?"

"Other than the guy was a Druid everything points to a normal life."

"Victim five, Richard Honeywell, car salesman, keen sportsman, ran Rowksly 46. Why was he found dead at an IT company? Do we believe he was enticed there in some way?"

"Yes, DI Lee."

"Everything about this guy was good, other than a blemish. People say he lied in court about a car that had failed for a customer, Jack Fernley. Mr Fernley a few years later committed suicide."

"Victim six, luckily this guy was saved from certain death."

"DS Yap, what can you tell us Martyn Bloom?"

"Well-known local window cleaner, bit of lad by all accounts. In the close where Mrs Lewis lived one lady said she suspected that they were having an affair. He was there twice a week, up to two hours at a time, and Mrs Lewis husband worked away."

"Has anybody spoken to Mr Lewis?"

"We checked Sir, and he is off Aberdeen. He is on the oil rigs for six weeks at a time. His supervisor said he is only three weeks into his latest stint, so we can count him out of the attack I think."

"Ok, they are our victims. Now the suspects."

PAY FOR YOUR SIN

"DI Milton, have you had any joy locating our ginger haired Jehovah Witness attacker?"

"I have checked at Micklock and Ackbourne, they have nobody fitting our description."

"What's everyone thoughts on our other suspects? Let's start with Cuthbert Lord?"

"Yes, DS Yap."

"Quite sure this guy isn't our killer, looking at history, bank accounts etc."

"Suspect two was Tommy Spire, but we all know how that ended. Suspect three, the elusive Dick."

"DI Smarty?"

"I say we keep him in. It's too much of a coincidence. He visits then she is killed."

"I agree, DI Smarty."

"Suspect four, Andrew Able."

"Yes, DI Lee."

"A definite candidate for me, Sir. He has all the trade marks."

"Suspect five, Alistair Mackay, any thoughts?"

"DS Winnipeg?"

"Think we have done him to death, Sir. I don't think he killed anyone."

"Ok, Suspect six, Rick Fernley."

"DS Bass?"

"I think this is our killer, he has motive and no alibi."

"Ok, so if we all agree, we pool our resources looking for the Jehovah's Witness, also the elusive Dick, the vicar Andrew Able and Rick Fernley. Close down the others but keep them on file."

"Right, DS Smarty and DS Bass take Andrew Able, watch him, keep tabs on his whereabouts, who he visits, who his friends are etc."

PAY FOR YOUR SIN

"DI Lee and DS Winnipeg, you do the same with Rick Fernley."

"DS Yap and DI Milton, I need you to find our Jehovah's witness and the elusive Dick if possible."

"Ok everyone, let's not have another attack. Thank you."

Gammon left the office and rang Phyllis Swann to see if she could get his Versace suit cleaned before Saturday. She was a diamond, she said she would take down today and have it back by Friday. And did he want his light blue John Rocha shirt ironing ready?

Phyllis knew John too well he thought. She even knew what he would wear with his suit. Not many cleaners like Phyllis Swann about he thought.

Gammon decided to go to Micklock, Kingdom Hall himself and speak with one of the group. Kingdom Hall was a new build perched on the side of Micklock Bank. A former dairy had stood there for many years until they bought the land, knocked the building down, and built a Kingdom Hall.

Gammon arrived just has two guys were coming out of the hall.

"Oh, hi I'm DCI Gammon, I wonder if I could ask you a few questions?

"Yes certainly, my friend," the taller of the two men said.

Once inside they took Gammon to a side room. He thought how very polite and respectful they were.

"I am looking for a ginger haired guy who may have been involved in a serious attack on a man yesterday. Sorry about the hair reference, but that's all we have to go on."

"I can't think of anybody that comes here, Mr Gammon."

PAY FOR YOUR SIN

"Well, it was a long shot."

"Just a minute though," the shorter guy said.

"What about Gary?"

"Gary Irwin?"

"Oh yeah, he is a ginger haired guy, only been with us about a year."

"Where can I find this Gary guy?"

"I am unsure. He works at the pet food factory in Dilley Dale."

"Is that the one that was a flour mill originally?"

"Yes, that's correct Mr Gammon, he helps out on his days off. He works four on, three off, I believe. He works continental shifts, spreading the word on his days off."

"I think he did live in Swinster, but I believe he lives in Cramford now."

"Ok, I will try and catch him at work today. Thanks for your help gentlemen," and Gammon left heading for the pet food mill in Dilley Dale.

The old flour mill, as Gammon knew it, had been where all the local farmers went for their feed for the winter. It had been in the same family for eight generations, but like all things eventually the interest was lost, and two guys bought it out. Richard Fearn and Michael Hufton.

Both nice guys by all accounts, they paid a decent rate and looked after their employees pretty well. Gammon went to the sales desk where a young lady in her mid-twenties greeted him.

"Hi DCI John Gammon," he said flashing his warrant card.

"I wonder if it would be possible to speak with Gary Irwin?"

"Yes, not a problem. I will put a call out for him."

PAY FOR YOUR SIN

"Gary Irwin to the sales desk please, Gary Irwin to the sales desk please."

After a few minutes a ginger haired guy in his mid-thirties arrived.

"Gary, this is DCI gammon from Bixton Police, he wishes to speak with you."

"Please feel free to use the back office."

Irwin didn't appear nervous or cocky to Gammon as they entered the back office with the clutter usually assigned to an office rarely used.

"Gary, take a seat."

Irwin sat down.

"Excuse my dusty overalls, Mr Gammon. I am on the powder plant today. How can I help you?"

"Where were you around 4.50pm last night?"

Irwin thought for a minute.

"I had left a house on Horsedale View, I believe it was number 37 and I was heading to Sydnope Street for my last few calls of the day."

"Did you by any chance meet a window cleaner before you got to Sydnope Street?"

Irwin went quiet.

"Gary, I will ask you again, did you see a window cleaner?"

"Yes, he was injured and there was a man running away. I think I disturbed him. I comforted the man then called the Police."

"What did you say?"

"I just said there is a man injured near Sydnope Street?"

"Did you say anything else? Gary, now is the time to speak."

"Yes, Mr Gammon. I said he survived."

"Why did you not wait with him and do it all properly?"

"Mr Gammon, I am thirty four years old. From seventeen until I found Jehovah I was a drug addict and I drank. I once beat a man half senseless just to get his bottle of whisky off him. I was jailed for four years. That's when I started studying and it's changed my life. I was scared it could all be ripped away from me."

"Look Gary, I have to take you in for further questioning at the station. You are not under arrest, and if everything checks out then I will speak to the owners and explain what happened, so you won't lose your job. Ok?"

Irwin nodded, and they left for Bixton.

On the way Gammon wasn't sure if this guy was telling the truth or not. He seemed very plausible, but he had been in the job long enough to know everything you think you see isn't always what you see."

Once back at the station Gammon instructed DI Smarty to take DNA saliva from Irwin. Gary Irwin didn't mind, which also made Gammon think that this guy was confident.

"So, Gary run through with me when you attacked the man for his whisky?"

Irwin cleared his throat.

"I was almost twenty nine and had been living rough for twelve years."

"Where are you from originally, Gary?"

"Manchester, I lived on the streets begging when I was kicked out of the house by my step-father. I don't blame him now. He just got sick of the way I was living my life, and now I am straight I can see why."

"Ok, going back to the attack?"

"It was a cold night. I only had thirty pence in begging money and I needed a drink. The guy in the next doorway had a good day and had bought a bottle of Jack Daniels. I asked him to share. The guy was about sixty I think. Anyway he wouldn't,

PAY FOR YOUR SIN

so I figured he wouldn't put up much of a
fight and I tried to take the bottle. What I
didn't realise was that he had been a
marine. He put up a hell of a fight but
being a younger age I won. I'm not proud
of this Mr Gammon, and I will carry this
guilt to my grave."

"I want you to look at these dates and
times and see if you can tell me of your
whereabouts please, Gary?"

Gammon passed over times of the
murders to Irwin.

"That first time and date I was off work
sick, so I was at home in Cramford."

"Did anybody see you at that time?"

"No, because I was sick Mr Gammon."

"Ok, look at the next time."

"I would have been on my way home
from work."

"How do you travel; bus, walk, car?"

"Car, Mr Gammon."

"So, would you have been anywhere near Puddle Dale on that date at about 5.30pm?"

"I can't remember, I don't think so though."

"What about this time? You look like you work out Gary?"

"I like running."

"Where do you run?"

"Oh everywhere, there are so many places, Mr Gammon."

"So, that time and date there, would you have been out running?"

"Quite possibly."

"Can you remember your route?"

"To be honest, no. I sometimes drive to a spot and run, and sometimes just set off from Cramford and run. It depends on how I feel."

"On this date did you see anybody else out and about?"

PAY FOR YOUR SIN

"Oh blimey, Mr Gammon, I often see quite a few people, it's quite popular."

"Try and think, Gary."

"Irwin sat for a minute.

"Actually, I remember seeing a guy with ginger hair, but he wasn't in running gear and he didn't appear to have a dog with him. I only noticed him because us gingers have to stick together, Mr Gammon," and Irwin laughed.

"Ok, what about this time and date?"

"I can't recollect anything on that date and time."

"Think, Gary."

Irwin again took his time but still said he couldn't remember.

"Finally, this date and time. Where were you?"

"I know I was at home at that time."

"Would anybody be able to back you up on that, Gary?"

"I doubt it, once I am in the house I don't go out. I never go to a bar or anything like that because of the temptation I just go to work, do my running and watch TV."

"Ok Gary, well thank you for your help. You are free to go although we may need you for a line up once Martyn Bloom is fit to identify his attacker."

"No bother, Mr Gammon, willing to help."

Irwin left the station and Gammon sat a moment. Some of the things Irwin had said about the ginger guy seemed like it was made up. Was this a way of him deflecting one of the killings found by Peter Gregory of Brichover. But then on the other hand he seemed very calm. He was either extremely confident or had nothing to do with the murders.

PAY FOR YOUR SIN

Saturday soon came around and John had booked to stay at Le Manoir Aux Quat Saisons, Raymond Blanc's hotel and restaurant, considered one of the best in the country. John had decided to see if he and Saron could get back together, and maybe something like this would add the romance.

They arrived at 2.30pm and a bell boy met them. John had really pushed the boat out and taken one of the grand rooms with a four poster bed and all the trappings a top hotel would have. Saron was suitably impressed, but her mother owned Trissington Hall which was equally impressive.

They had only been in the room fifteen minutes when John's mobile rang. It was Graham Swann.

"Good afternoon, John."

"Good afternoon, Sir."

"I'm afraid my wife Marilyn isn't well. I have to cancel tonight's celebration. I hope this won't upset your plans too much, thought I best call you before you set off."

"Understand Sir, I hope your wife is better very soon."

"Thank you, John. I will speak soon," and Swann hung up.

John explained to Saron what had happened. It sounded like a lame excuse with him not saying to Swann that they were already in Oxfordshire, but it was the truth.

"So now what, John?"

"Well it would be a shame to waste all this. I will book us a table in the restaurant tonight. What shall we do this afternoon?"

John looked at Saron in her tight denim leggings, high heeled calf boots and tight light blue blouse and she knew what he was thinking.

PAY FOR YOUR SIN

"You can get that thought out of your head, John Gammon," she said with a wry smile.

"You do me an injustice, Saron. So what would you like to do?"

"I would love to go and see the Cotswolds."

"Ok, our evening meal is booked for 8.30m so we have enough time. Bourton on the Water was a beautiful little village. It was a bit more commercialised than John could remember when he was taken there by his mother on a Hittington Women's Institute trip, but still very pleasant. And what mattered to John was Saron was really enjoying it. Had he got the guts to ask if they could get back together? He decided that he would ask that night.

It was almost 6.30pm when they arrived back at their accommodation. It was just going dark and the driveway was lit up.

"John, it's like a fairy tale isn't it?"

"Guess so," John replied trying to sound positive.

They showered and changed. John in his suit, and Saron in a white dress cut at the leg with a silver trim and she wore silver kitten heeled shoes.

"You look fabulous, you really do."

"Thank you, John," she said with that seductive smile that melted John like no other woman could.

They headed down to the plush dining room. This was going to be a world class gastronomic delight. Saron got a lot of admiring looks as glided between the tables to the table we were to be seated at.

The table had a plush white table with a small vase holding what John thought were three purple orchids. Everything about the settings was exquisite. John had ordered the set course evening menu. He ordered a bottle of Chablis Premier Cruz for the following courses for them both; Cornish crab kaffir lime with coconut and passion fruit followed by Cornish lamb courgette, Jersey Royals and preserved lemon and for dessert coconut and dark chocolate Granada grand cru.

"That was excellent, John. I really enjoyed it."

The waiter arrived and took their plates and dishes away, but came back with a cheese board the like of which neither had seen before. It was a silver platter with Taleggio which the waiter said was a spongy type Italian cheese. Cotija, a Mexican salty cheese, French Roquefort, Greek Feta, English Cheddar, French Camembert and Spanish Manchego. All was complimented with red grapes, cherries, strawberries and blueberries with every type of cracker you could imagine.

They finished what they could before thanking the waiter and heading for their room. Saron said she needed the bathroom. John poured them a glass of Cristal he had ordered for the room and lay in bed.

She appeared out of the bathroom naked, her silky skin radiant in the soft lighting of the room. They lay in bed talking.

"Can I say something, John?"

"Of course."

"Please, this isn't that I don't fancy you, but I need to get my head straight. We can sleep together but no naughty stuff. Is that ok?"

John was a bit surprised at Saron's stance. He hadn't allowed for that, so now did he say anything about getting back together? Saron lay her head on his chest and her blonde hair cascading down.

"I know what this is all about, John. I am flattered that you have taken so much care to get me here and treat me like you have, but yesterday I was told you had a child with Anouska. Is that true?"

John almost dropped his glass.

"If it's true John, then the baby was probably conceived on the eve of what should have been our wedding night."

"Who is saying these things?"

John knew if he didn't lie Saron was lost forever, and from that point they would just be friends.

"This isn't true, Saron."

"If I find you have lied to me John, I will never trust you again. I don't want to ruin the evening so I'm going to sleep," and she rolled over onto her side. Who the hell told Saron about his child with Anouska he thought? Things were stacking up against him. First Steve and India, and now Saron and the baby with Anouska. It was not like John to lie, in fact he hated it, but he could not see a choice at the minute. Needless to say he didn't get a lot of sleep before it was time to get up.

"You ok John? You look tired."

"Oh, just work."

"You never switch off, you know that. The pub is the same, but I promised myself that I would forget it this weekend. I have had a lovely time, really nice, thank you," and she kissed John.

John wanted to hold her but thought best not to push his luck. The one thing he was thinking might get him out of the mess, was to try and get a DNA test done on the baby. If it turned out she wasn't his, then he would be in the clear.

PAY FOR YOUR SIN

They had breakfast although neither of them ate much after the sumptuous meal the previous night. John paid the bill and they left, taking a nice steady drive back to Derbyshire. Everything felt right John thought, so he made his mind up to sort the Anouska thing. If she was his then he would come clean with Saron and what happens happens he thought.

They arrived back at just gone 4.00pm and Saron told John she was going to relieve Donna so she could have the night off.

John kissed her, thanked for a lovely weekend and headed home to the cottage. Once at home he showered poured a Jameson's and made himself a sandwich and sat going through his e-mails. Half way down the fifty e-mails was one from Fleur.

'Hi John, if its ok with you I will land at East Midlands airport on Wednesday. Can you pick me up or should I get a hire car? Reply to me on this number then discard it'.

John knew what kind of job Fleur did but the intrigue often made him smile.

John replied on the mobile number.

'Will struggle to pick you up. Get a hire car and I will leave you a key behind the log store on a nail. Looking forward to seeing you. Love John xx'

That was a bit of good news he thought.

PAY FOR YOUR SIN

CHAPTER SEVEN

The following morning he headed for work calling at Beryl's Butties for a doorstep bacon sandwich and a strong black coffee, that only this café could make to John's liking. It was quite full, mainly with lorry drivers, so John stood out a bit in his work clothes, but he wasn't bothered as long as he got his sandwich and coffee.

He finished his breakfast, paid the bill and left. He was almost at work when his mobile rang.

"Saron, you ok?"

"Yes, fine John, just wondered if you wanted to come with me Sunday afternoon to Pritwich Hall. Lola and Chris are doing a champagne afternoon tea thing to get to know everybody."

John couldn't believe his luck.

"Would love to. What time shall I pick you up?"

"2.00pm would be good."

"Ok, look forward to it."

"Bye John," and she hung up.

John could hardly hold his delight then he remembered Fleur was coming Wednesday. Then again, she could be gone by Sunday he thought.

"Everything good, Magic?"

"Yes Sir, Di Trimble said she had a quiet night last night."

"Good, that's how we want it."

Smarty and Milton were just coming down stairs.

"You got minute lads?"

Gammon took them back to the office.

"Gary Irwin, I interviewed him. I think it would be a good idea to keep a watch on him, so you know my next proposition. One of you, twelve hour nights, one

PAY FOR YOUR SIN

twelve hour days for a week lads please.
You two sort between yourselves. I want
the day guy to call me at 8.30am with a
full report even if it's nothing. Thanks."

Smarty and Milton left John's office.

Here we go again he thought;
paperwork. He hated it with a passion, but
it had to be done. He was halfway down
the pile when there was a knock on his
door. It was DS Winnipeg.

"Can I have a word, Sir?"

"Of course John, come in pull up a chair.
How can I help you?"

"Well Sir, my girlfriend applied for a
higher position in the NHS and she got it."

"Ok, where is it?"

"Liverpool, and she wants us to get
married and me to move with her."

"Oh right, have you applied to
Merseyside police?"

"I wasn't being sneaky Sir, but yes I have, and they have a position I can transfer to."

"Ok, when?"

"That's the hard bit, next week."

"Look John, these things happen. I could do without losing you. You have been a good DI for me, but I fully understand you want to be with your future wife, so I won't stand in your way."

"Sir, I can't tell you how pleased she will be. Thank you for being so understanding."

Gammon stood up and shook Winnipeg's hand.

"All the very best. Just one thing, you have to arrange a leaving party at the Spinning Jenny. It's tradition."

"I'll get on it now, Sir."

PAY FOR YOUR SIN

Gammon stood looking to Losehill. Losing a DS wasn't the best thing to happen.

It was almost 5.00pm so John called Kev.

"Hey retired man, do you fancy a quick one in the Spinning Jenny?"

"Always got time for that John. Pick me up on the way up and Doreen will fetch me back."

"Ok mate, will be about 5.40pm."

"Great, see you then."

Gammon finished off what he was doing and headed out to pick Kev up. John pulled up at Kev's and he was outside waiting dressed in his chequered golfing trousers and a pink collared tee shirt.

"Looking very dandy, old lad," John said as Kev got in the car.

"Been golfing with Jack Etchings at Cramford Country Club. Won eighteen pounds off him, he wasn't pleased," and Kev laughed.

"Do you fancy one at The Black Bess at Biffington by Hittington for a change, John? Then we can go back to the Spinning Jenny."

"Can do mate."

Last time John was in there was with India on Christmas Day.

They walked in and the landlord recognised John.

"Blimey, your partner isn't as good looking as the one Christmas Day son."

John smiled.

"Two pints of Goose-head."

"Does he know, John?"

"Not really, just popped in for a quick one on Christmas Day."

"Who, with Saron?"

"You guess."

PAY FOR YOUR SIN

John thought that answer was better than lying.

"Always knew you and Saron would get back together some day. Pleased for you lad. Now bloody behave, don't lose her again or you might not get another chance."

They sat in a corner near the fire.

"Nice pint this is, John. Was it busy Christmas Day?

"Not that bad, mate."

Always loved Christmas in the pub. The takings were good and everyone was always happy through that period.

"You were thinking of the jing jing of the till my friend," and John laughed.

They had two pints and decided to head back to the Spinning Jenny when the door opened, and Steve Lineman came in with India Green. Both Kev and John stood open mouthed. Not only was this a shock but to see Steve with India, who was the double of Jo, it just blew them away.

"What you drinking, Steve?"

"I'll have a pint of Ghost Tipple please."

"Would you two like a drink?" India said turning to John and Kev.

"No, we are fine love. We are heading back now."

John could sense the relief etched on Steve's face.

"I'll give you a call John, tomorrow."

"Ok, mate."

Kev and John left both still in shock, Kev more than John.

"Is he seeing that lady, John? He hasn't been married two minutes. I thought it was Jo, she is her double."

"There is a fair chance she is Jo's twin sister, Kev. She was adopted as a baby and moved here to write a book and try to find her roots."

PAY FOR YOUR SIN

"Bloody hell, that will put the cat among the pigeons, mate."

"Tell me about it, Kev."

All John could hope for was the gobby landlord didn't say anything to Steve about John being in the pub Christmas night, or that would light the blue touch paper and who knows where that could end.

Back at the Spinning Jenny John had forewarned Kev to keep it to himself about Steve and India. He said he would. Phil Sterndale and Sheba Filey were sitting at the bar. They had been in the restaurant for a meal.

"How was it, mate?"

"Yes, good John. They seem a nice couple and the standards are being kept. Lyndsay is a very good cook, and Wez seems to have taken to the bar. Well, his Pedigree is spot on, mate. Let me get you two one."

"Hey Wez, two pints of Pedigree for these two reprobates please."

"This is good Phil. Thanks," John said as he took the top off his creamy pint.

"Are you two going to Pritwich Hall on Sunday for that party thing that Lola and Chris are doing?"

"I know me and Doreen are going. What about you, John?"

"Yes, I'll be there, going with Saron."

"Oh, is it back on then?"

"Good friends, Sheba."

"Yeah, like John Gammon has just good friends. Pull the other one."

Phil almost fell off his stool he was laughing so much.

"Told you the past would catch up with you, John lad."

"What's this? Get at John night, Kev!"

PAY FOR YOUR SIN

"You have to pay for everything in life my son," and Kev and Phil started laughing again.

"Sorry John, shouldn't have started that," and then Sheba laughed.

"Give me another three Pedigrees please Wez, that might shut them up."

"What you drinking, Sheba?"

"Bacardi and Coke please, John."

"Bacardi and Coke for the lady please, Wez."

Doreen arrived at 11.10pm to take Kev home, so they wrapped up the night. On the way home John was thinking if Fleur could help with the Anouska thing.

It was Wednesday and John was looking forward to the arrival of Fleur. She had rung to say she was at the cottage and did he want to meet her somewhere to eat. He suggested Up The Step's Maggie's at 6.00pm.

John was going through what DI Milton had reported on Gary Irwin. Smarty had told Milton that Irwin kept some strange hours. He came home around 9.00pm and then wasn't seen until almost 3.30am when he came out of his garage in his car. Smarty had followed and Irwin had driven to a picnic site near Cramford. Smarty said he abandoned his car for fear of spooking him. Irwin waited on a picnic table and a set of car lights drove in. They threw a plastic bag towards Irwin then drove on, but Smarty could not get the car registration or make of car. He said he followed Irwin back to his house. He said a light was on in the kitchen until Irwin left again at 6.45 am for work.

What should Gammon do? Did he bring him back in to talk about what Smarty had seen? Did he leave it a few more days? He decided the latter was best.

John drove to the pub to meet Fleur. She was already sitting at a table with a glass of Buxton Spring water.

"Hey John."

She stood up and they embraced.

"How are you?"

"Yeah, good Fleur, been so excited since you said you were coming."

"So, do you have a lady in your life?"

"Kind of."

"Let me guess; the lovely Saron."

"Am I that transparent?"

"You will never get her out of your system."

They ordered two Maggie specials, bangers and mash with onion gravy and cheese dipped asparagus, a pub speciality.

Over dinner John told Fleur about Anouska and the baby, and his concern if Saron ever found out.

"Give me all the details of where this woman lives. I will need a sample of your DNA John, and I will tell you if this child is definitely yours. Or if not, I will possibly be able to tell you who is the father."

"Thank you, Fleur. I have one more favour."

He explained about India Green and could she do some research to see if her story stacks up about being adopted, and being the identical twin sister of Jo. Fleur said that would not be a problem.

With the meal finished they decided to go back to the cottage. It was almost 10.30pm and John asked Fleur if she wanted a night cap, and what was she doing tomorrow. She said she had a

PAY FOR YOUR SIN

meeting in Derby but could not divulge what it was about.

"Ok, goodnight then Fleur. I will see you tomorrow night."

They both headed for bed.

The following morning John showered and shaved and headed for Bixton Fleur was still in bed when he left.

He had mulled over the Gary Irwin situation and decided to get a search warrant for his house. When he arrived at work DI Smarty was waiting for him.

"Morning, Sir."

"Good morning, Dave. I thought you were doing the nightshift watch on Irwin."

"That's what I need to talk to you about."

"Here grab a coffee and come up to my office."

"I need to tell you this. Last night Irwin went out around 10.00pm. I discreetly followed him, and he went to what looked like an old scout hut in Pritwich. I parked out of the way when I saw cars arriving; five in total with Irwin's. I sneaked round the back and I could just hear some of the conversations. Pretty sure Irwin and another guy whose voice I didn't recognise were leading the meeting. I heard him say Gammon is suspicious. Then the other guy said we need to complete our task, do we all agree? They all said yes and clapped.

I heard one of them say, 'They Pay For Their Sin'!"

"The meeting went on for another ten or fifteen minutes then they came out. Because it was dark I struggled to get to see any car registrations and all bloody cars look alike these days. I got one John. It was D11 FMP on a C Class Mercedes."

PAY FOR YOUR SIN

"Well done Dave. Get off home, you must be knackered. Don't bother tonight I'm calling the surveillance off from today. I have enough to search Irwin's house and it sounds like he is part of some kind of cult. Come back in tomorrow as usual and thanks again great work."

Gammon called Milton and explained what had happened. He said to stay at Irwin's house as he was getting a search warrant and would be bringing Irwin in if they found anything incriminating.

Gammon rallied his staff. DS Bass, DI Lee, DS Yap and Wally's team headed for Irwin's house. On entry they could smell something quite nasty. He had left what looked like a sheep's head on the stove boiling. It was gross. DS Bass had to go outside to be physically sick. Gammon turned it off.

"Carl, did Irwin leave for work this morning?"

"Yes Sir, I followed him, and he was at work."

"Ok, get over there, let's have him back in for questioning. Tell him he needs a solicitor please, Carl."

"Will do, Sir."

The house didn't give up any evidence, so they moved to the garden and the greenhouse and garden shed.

"Sir, got something."

DI Lee appeared with what looked like a scalpel knife.

"Give it to Wally please, Peter. We may have something."

Gammon was hoping for the brown envelope Smarty had seen being thrown toward Irwin at the picnic site a couple of nights previous. Gammon was in no doubts that Irwin had something to hide.

PAY FOR YOUR SIN

"Ok, everyone except Wally's team back to the station."

"John, I have left Denise in the lab just get her to swab this scalpel. We are looking for any DNA from the victims."

"Ok, thanks Wally, will see you in a bit."

Gammon returned to the station and gave Denise the scalpel and told her to disturb him when she knew anything. He would be in interview room two with Gary Irwin and his solicitor.

Gammon entered the room with DI Lee. Milton was already on the recording machine. Gammon nodded to him to introduce everyone.

"Ok, Mr Lewis or Gary?"

"Gary is fine. I just want to know what I have done?"

"You spoke to my client already, and I am told you have searched his house, Inspector."

Gammon looked at Irwin's solicitor with total disdain. He was going to correct him now he was acting Chief Constable, but thought it wasn't worth the effort.

"Ok Gary, we have searched your house today. Can you tell me what the sheep's head was being boiled for?"

"It's the eyes, Mr Gammon. We boil them. I like to eat them with sardines on toast."

Gammon felt like throwing up.

"Are you a member of any club or cult society, Gary?"

Gary spoke in his solicitor's ear guarding his mouth with his hand.

"No," he replied.

"Are you sure about that answer, Gary?"

"Yes," he replied again but this time in an aggressive tone.

"Can you explain your whereabouts between 9.00pm and 11.00pm last night?"

PAY FOR YOUR SIN

"I was at home."

"So, you are telling me you never left your house?"

"Correct," he said again in an aggressive tone.

"We have been watching your whereabouts Gary, and one of my officers followed you last night between those times stated. You went to a scout hut in Pritwich and met with more people. Would you like to tell me what that was about?"

"None of your business."

"Well I intend to make it my business, Gary, so I will ask you again.

Again, Irwin said, "None of your business."

"Well Gary, at the search, which incidentally is still in operation, with my forensic team found a scalpel, they type used in operating theatres. Would you know anything about that? Before you answer, it is being analysed for any DNA from the victims found with 'RPF' found carved in their feet."

Irwin laughed.

"So, you think my tomato knife is a killer's weapon, Mr Gammon? Do I look that stupid?

"I would rather not comment on that statement, Gary."

Just then Denise called Gammon out of the room.

"Sir, there was a very small amount of blood that had seeped into where the blade sits in the handle, but I'm afraid not enough to get DNA from or anything to be honest."

Damn Gammon thought.

"Ok Denise, thanks for you quick appraisal."

PAY FOR YOUR SIN

Gammon went back in the room and Milton started the tape again.

Gary, we have found blood on the scalpel taken from your greenhouse. Now who do you think the blood came from?"

"I would guess a tomato plant, Mr Gammon."

"Let me tell you what I think, Gary Iriwn. I think you are up to your neck in this. I also think you would be wise to give up your fellow friends before it's too late. I will get enough evidence to charge you at some point and it would be better for you to come clean now."

Irwin smirked in a confident way.

"Are you charging my client Mr Gammon, or are we free to go?"

"If your client doesn't wish to save his own skin then by all means leave, but I will throw the book at him eventually."

Gammon turned to Milton to turn off the tape as Irwin and his solicitor left the room.

Gammon sat with Lee and Milton.

"It's him lads, we just have to prove it."

Carl explain to Dave we need him watching again tonight. He will slip up eventually."

"Do you want me there in the day, Sir?"

"Yes please, Carl."

Gammon left the room cursing his luck.

The next four days it was clear Irwin knew he was being watched. It was now Sunday and the champagne tea at Pritwich Hall.

Gammon picked up Saron. She had a short brown leather skirt with a light purple silk blouse, as always looking absolutely perfect in John's eyes.

Chris and Lola had put two big marquees on the back lawn; one with a jazz band playing and the other with a disco playing. Saron said she fancied listening to the jazz for a while. Shelley and Jack were in there, so they sat with them.

"Oh John, you have to try these prawn vol-au-vents. I think they have Greek yogurt in them."

Shelley passed John and Saron the silver server adorned with every vol-au-vent you could imagine.

"Wow Shelley, they are special, aren't they?"

"I thought you might like them Saron. Bloody lovely, that's what they are," and Shelley laughed.

"Who has done the catering for Chris and Lola?"

"Cheryl and Jackie."

"Well I have to say this is impressive."

Typical Shelley straight in with her size ten.

"You should have them when you decide to tie the knot again."

John could feel the uneasiness of the situation.

"That isn't going to happen, Shelley!"

"Oh, sorry love, I wasn't prying, just you are such the perfect couple and your kids would be amazing."

"Keep digging," Jack said as he tried to change the subject seeing this wasn't going to well.

"Hey Cheryl, superb buffet."

"Thanks Jack. Me and Jackie worked really hard, we are hoping to get some new business from it. Chris has a lot of business contacts that will be here today."

"Have you been in the other marquee yet?"

"Yes, just left Bob dancing with Tracey Rodgers. He is almost falling over his

PAY FOR YOUR SIN

tongue and if his eyes pop out much more they will be in Swinster."

"He is having a good time then?"

"Just a bit John, you know Bob when he has had a drink."

"I have to see this. Come on Saron, let's have a dance."

John and Saron headed to the disco marquee. Sure enough, Bob was in full flight twirling Tracey round to 'You Spin Me Right Round'.

Next up was 'Dancing Queen' by Abba. John wasn't too keen but Saron wanted to dance. She could see Bob making a bee line for her, so she grabbed John's arm and took him on the dance floor.

"Getting rough with me there, Saron," and he laughed.

"It was either that or have Bob twirling me round on the dance floor like a whirling dervish," and she laughed.

After a few dances Chris stood up to thank everyone for coming.

"We thought it would be a bit of fun if we did a Mr and Mrs thing, which I'm sure you are all game for. So I would like Bib and Cheryl, Tony and Rita from our local pub, Jack and Shelley Etchings and we just need one more couple."

Bob shouted John and Saron. John waved his hand.

"No, we are ok."

"Oh, come on don't be a dry bread," Shelley said. Before they knew what was what they were on the stage.

"I will compare," Chris said. "Lola will put the headphones and blindfold the players. The prize is a week on my yacht in the Bahamas. I will pay to fly you out, all expenses paid by me."

A big cheer went up from everyone in the marquee.

PAY FOR YOUR SIN

Jack and Shelley went first and scored five out of eight questions.

"Well done you two, that's a big score to beat."

Next up Bob and Cheryl. Cheryl went first and got four out of four correct.

"She knows you, Pants on Yer Head Bob," some wag in the tent shouted.

Now it was Bob's turn. He managed two, so they took the lead. Now it was Rita and Tony's turn. They scored the same as Bob and Cheryl, so were tying for first place. Next up was John and Saron. Saron answered the questions first.

"Ok Saron, what is John's pet hate?"

She thought for a minute.

"Wet towels."

"Ok. His favourite dinner?"

"Oh, that's easy, Beef Stroganoff."

If I said to John would you play cricket for the local team what would be his answer?"

"No, he would find an excuse. He's not a cricket fan."

"If I asked John would he like children, what would be his answer?"

"No, not ready."

"Well that was emphatic, Saron.

"Ok, now your turn John. What would most annoy Saron? Leaving the top of the toothpaste, a crying baby or a messy kitchen."

"Messy kitchen."

"If I asked Saron to name her favourite vegetable what would it be?"

"Cabbage."

"Ok now, if I had a portion of cheesecake or apple pie, which would she go for?"

John thought for a minute.

PAY FOR YOUR SIN

"Apple Pie, I think."

"What books does she like to read, Thriller, Romance or history?"

"Ok, because it's all so close we are going to ask Saron to confirm John's answers first?"

Saron answered, "Messy kitchen."

"Ok, one correct. Next one."

"Sweetcorn."

"Oh Saron, that's wrong, he said it was cabbage. Third question. Romance, well done to John, Saron said romance was the third answer. Apple pie, brilliant that, was Saron's answer."

"Great John, you got three out of four on Saron's answers. Now John it's all on you, so no pressure."

"The first answer Saron gave for John was?"

John said, "Wet towels."

"Brilliant, that's correct. Next question; John what would you have for your favourite dinner?"

"Beef Stroganoff."

"That's another point now. You two are at five, last two right and you win. If asked I you to play cricket for the village team would your answer be, yes or no?"

"Yes, I would play but I'm not very good."

"Oh John, she said no. Ok now the final answer. Get this right and we have a tie break between three of you. Ok, I asked Saron if you would say you would like children, and your answer is John?"

"Yes, I would love children."

"Oh John, she said no."

Saron wasn't pleased but couldn't show it.

The sudden death question for Tony and Rita, Bob and Cheryl was; who was the

PAY FOR YOUR SIN

first man to sail solo round the world? Immediately Rita put her hand up.

"Robin Knox Johnston."

"The winners are Tony and Rita."

Cheryl was mumbling that the question was unfair has Rita had been a sailor.

Saron suddenly said she wanted to go home.

"Are you feeling ill?"

"Just take me home John, this was a mistake."

"What have I done?"

"Just take me home."

John found Chris and Lola and thanked them for a pleasant afternoon but Saron wasn't feeling well.

On the way back to the Tow'd Man Saron never spoke.

"I'll come in," John said as they pulled onto the car park.

"You needn't bother," she said as she got out of the car.

"Saron, what have I done?"

"I didn't think you were ready for children, but your answer said it all. I mean you already have one with that slapper. I hope you will both be very happy," and she slammed the car door and headed inside the pub.

"Women, I will never understand them." He arrived back at the cottage to a note on the table.

'Had to leave John. I am sorry but work calls. I have taken your toothbrush for DNA. I will be in touch about Anouska.'

John was thinking to himself that it didn't matter. He had lost Saron because of all this.

PAY FOR YOUR SIN

Another week in work and Gammon was staring out of his window towards Losehill, when an excited Wally came in.

"John, good news, I have a DNA sample from a bed sheet we took from Amy Lord. Just by chance we took the bed sheet and it wasn't spotted at first."

"Who is it, Wally?"

"Only bloody Gary Irwin."

"Really?"

Gammon picked up the phone to DI Lee.

"Peter, get me Gary Irwin in now. I am going to charge him. I have DNA. Make sure he has his solicitor."

Gammon was feeling excited; a break through at last.

"DS Yap, good news. We've got Irwin's DNA on the bed sheet of Amy Lord."

"Well I have some other good news. I have found the owner of the Merc, Sir. It's a Michael Luton, and he works with Irwin."

"Get him in now for questioning please, Ian."

Everything yesterday with Saron was paling into insignificance. He had the feeling the case was about to explode.

Gammon decided to make Irwin sweat and decided to question Michael Luton first.

Luton was a small weedy guy with horn rimmed glasses. Gammon got the interview started as DS Bass started the recording.

"Mr Luton, I'm DCI Gammon, may I call you Michael?"

Luton was very nervous and nodded.

"Your Mercedes was seen at a picnic site in Cramford in the early hours of the morning at some kind of meeting. What can you tell me about the meeting, Michael?"

Luton was quiet but the suddenly said, "I want to tell you everything for a deal. This is my solicitor."

Luton handed Gammon a piece of paper with the name Lloyd Andrews. Gammon immediately got Magic to ring Andrews and he said he was in Bixton. and would be a few minutes.

Andrews arrived and Gammon restarted the meeting.

"So Michael, you wish to tell us everything?"

"Yes."

"Please feel free."

"The meeting is held every two weeks. The members are called the good people. There are nine members and to be a member you have to take back the sinner's life."

"Explain to me, Michael."

"Well that's what I want to explain, but first can I be immune from prosecution?"

"Have you killed anybody, Michael?"

"No, but it is my turn next."

"Ok, so you have only attended meetings?"

"Yes."

"Well I can speak up for you. Now you have turned Queen's evidence it will be in your favour. At worst maybe four years and you will be out in eighteen months. Depending on the time it takes to get to trial, your remand time will be taken into account."

"Who are the people responsible for the murders?"

"Amy Lord was Gary Irwin. He is one of the leaders. She was killed because she committed adultery. The second killing

PAY FOR YOUR SIN

was Annie Board. She was killed for stealing in the sixties."

"Who killed Annie Board?"

"Richard Freestone."

"That answers the Dick visit mentioned by Margaret Staffy."

"The third victim was Freeman Gillespie because he operated on the Sabbath."

"Can I hold you there. Is this a religious sect?"

"Kind of, Mr Gammon."

"Who killed Mr Gillespie?"

"Tobias Wilcox. The fourth killing was Hayden Tusker killed by Maurice Crocker. Trusper was a Druid and it says in the bible you can only have one God. Number five was Richard Honeywell. He bore false witness against Rick Fernley, so his brother Jack was allowed to kill him. Victim six went wrong. Martyn Bloom had coveted another man's wife. Jimmy

Denn was disturbed, so I am quite sure they will kill him very soon."

"So, you said there were nine members? I need names please?"

The other three were me and Terry Ling and the leader was Richard Fearn."

"How did you all meet?"

"We all work for Richard and his partner Michael Hufton, but he had nothing to do with this."

"So why was RPF etched into the victim's feet?"

"It was Richard Fearn's idea. He said we could make it look like a serial killer and they would not look for all of us."

"But there were three letters on the feet 'R.P.F"

"Yes, Richard Paul Fearn."

"Hold it there."

PAY FOR YOUR SIN

Gammon went outside and told Magic to get all available officers to bring these men in with solicitors immediately.

Gammon went back in the room.

"So, you do know you will have to stand up in court against these men, don't you Michael?"

"Yes, but that's better than killing somebody."

During the following days Gammon charged all nine men. Seven with murder, one with attempted murder and Michael Luton with being party to the whole cult.

Richard Paul Fearn had been some kind of Svengali with these men. Gammon believed once Irwin had killed the first the other were frightened and assumed they were guilty by association. That's what the 'RPF' was for. To frighten the men to stay in line when they were killing and etching

'RPF' in the victim's foot, in their mind their master was in charge.

With one of his biggest cases put to bed Gammon arranged a celebration at the Spinning Jenny and fully expected to be given the Chief Constable position very soon instead of acting Chief Constable.

After a good night with everyone at the Spinning Jenny, John got in at 12.10am. He quickly showered and went to bed, only to be woken by a withheld number on his mobile.

"John, it's Fleur. I realise it's late, but I thought I best call you. I have the result of the DNA. Are you sitting down?"

"Anouska didn't take much finding. She lives in a bedsit in a small town in Latvia called Gronk. She appears to have a partner, but I can't be sure of that. What I can be sure of is the DNA result, John."

PAY FOR YOUR SIN

John held his breath. A part of him wanted the child to be his, but the other part wanted Saron and it was never going to happen if this child was his.

This DNA result could change John's life forever.

To be continued………..

Printed in Great Britain
by Amazon